JESSICA BECK
THE DONUT MYSTERIES, BOOK 43
BLENDED BRIBES

1

The First Time Ever Published!

The 43rd Donuts Mystery

Jessica Beck is the New York Times Bestselling Author of the Donut Mysteries, the Cast Iron Cooking Mysteries, the Classic Diner Mysteries, the Ghost Cat Cozy Mysteries, and more.

AS SUZANNE HART IS coming home from visiting her college roommate, Autumn, she spots smoke in the sky above downtown April Springs, North Carolina. She fears that either her donut shop or the cottage she shares with her husband, Jake, is on fire, but it turns out to be ReNEWed, Gabby Williams's gently used clothing shop next door to Donut Hearts. As Suzanne watches in horror, a fireman pulls someone from inside the burning building. Is it Gabby, and if it is, is she still alive? Only time will tell. As events begin to unfold, Suzanne and Grace do their best to uncover who would want to torch Gabby's business, and the owner along with it!

To P and E,

Forever and Always.

Chapter 1

First I saw the smoke climbing into the air above town, a massive plume of black that seemed intent on devouring the fading blue sky surrounding it as dusk began to near.

Then I smelled the foul stench of something burning that should never be on fire.

As I drove past the City Limits sign for April Springs, I finally heard the sirens.

I'd been away from home visiting my college roommate and helping her deal with the turmoil in her own life, but now I was coming home for a bit of peace and tranquility.

Or so I thought at the time.

Was it possible that Donut Hearts was on fire? After all, a great many flammable things occurred in my kitchen in order to bring folks their delightful treats every day. Between the massive fryer filled with scalding hot oil and the large coffee urns, there was enough potential danger in the place to make it an OSHA nightmare.

Had the dark specter of doom finally killed my life's ambition to be a donutmaker for the rest of my days?

Then again, if it *wasn't* my shop, it could just as easily have been my cottage, not a hundred yards from Donut Hearts as the crow flew. I'd grown up there with my mother and father, moved away to live with my first husband, Max, and then I'd come back again after that marriage had crumbled. Momma and I had shared the space until she'd found love again in the form of our former chief of police, Phillip Martin, and I'd been there alone until I'd married Jake, my second husband and the true love of my life. Was he all right? I couldn't bear not knowing as I raced toward the visions of chaos ahead of me.

It was all I could do to keep my Jeep on the road as I raced down Viewmont Avenue and onto Springs Drive, nearly running up on the sidewalk in front of city hall as I made the sharp turn to see what exactly was on fire.

Chapter 2

I nearly collided with a police cruiser as I made the sharp turn.
Slamming on my brakes, I managed to stop just in time before I
hit Officer Darby Jones. He was a big man, though not fat, and his eyes
grew wide when I came so close to running him down.

But that wasn't what my focus was on at the time.

It wasn't Donut Hearts that was on fire, but it was close.

Gabby Williams's shop, ReNEWed, was aflame, and as I started to
get out of my Jeep, I saw a fireman coming out of the back of the building with someone thrown over his back in a classic carry.

If I had to guess, I would have said that it was most likely Gabby being carried, and from the look of things, I couldn't be sure at all if she'd
managed to survive the fire or not.

"What happened?" I asked Darby after I climbed out. I tried to get
past him to see how Gabby was doing, but he didn't budge.

"Stay right where you are, Suzanne."

"She's my friend!" I protested. "She needs me!"

In a voice much calmer than mine had just been, Darby said, "If
you get in their way, you'll be hurting, not helping. If she's *really* your
friend, you'll stay right where you are."

I couldn't argue with his logic, as much as I might have wanted to.
All I could do was stand there and watch as the paramedics worked to
revive Gabby. I knew they were doing their best to save her, and as I
watched, the roof of her gently used clothing shop collapsed in on itself,

the flames leaping higher and higher into the evening air. Though the town's fire truck was doing its best to make a dent in the fire, the volunteer crew—no matter how skilled they might be—were clearly overmatched by the blazing inferno. On the other side of ReNEWed, and away from Donuts Hearts, the building where Patty Cakes had been located before shutting its doors for good was in danger of being engulfed as well, but what I was concerned with was what was on my side of the clothing shop.

That was my place, the converted train depot that now housed the business I'd bought after my painful divorce from Max.

They were starting to spray the side of my building as well.

One thing was certain: Gabby's business was gone, even if they did manage to put out the flames, which I thought was an impossible task, given the massive amount of clothing that had been stored inside it. The water and smoke damage alone would destroy the value of anything they might be able to save from the flames. The truth was that it was probably better to just let it burn to the ground, as hard as that was to even consider. I wasn't sure that I'd be that casual if Donut Hearts had been the business on fire at the moment, but I knew a total loss when I saw one.

Not that it would matter to anyone concerned if Gabby didn't manage to pull through.

"What happened?" Jake asked as he joined me. I hadn't even seen him approach, I'd been so mesmerized by what was happening. My husband put his arm around me and hugged me, all the while staring at the fire himself.

"I don't know. I just got here."

"Who is that they are working on?" He gestured.

"My guess is that it's Gabby," I told him. "I missed you," I added almost as an afterthought.

"I missed you, too," he said as he hugged me briefly again. "Good. At least they're hosing Donut Hearts and Patty Cakes down. At this point, that's about the best they can do." He shook his head as he looked at the blaze between them. What was left of ReNEWed was still shooting flames skyward despite the amount of water that was being directed at it, and I knew that it wouldn't be long before the only thing left was a pile of ashes.

"I guess," I said absently.

"Well, at least it's something," Jake said as they transferred the woman the fireman had pulled out of the flames onto a gurney and moved her into a nearby waiting ambulance. The brave fireman finally took off his helmet and mask, and I was surprised to see that it was the fire chief himself. Harley Lane hadn't been a young man in donkey's years, and if you had asked me earlier if I thought he was capable of carrying someone out of a roaring fire, I would have strongly doubted it, but I'd seen it for myself. He got as far as Donut Hearts before he slumped over into one of the chairs we kept out front for our al fresco diners.

I tried to rush over to him to see if I could help, but Darby just shook his head. "I'm sorry. I've got my orders," he said.

I wouldn't be able to do the chief any good, anyway. Besides, three of his men who weren't directly involved in dealing with the fire were tending to him, so I knew that he was in good hands. After a few moments, he shook them all off and stood, not even wavering for an instant. When he spotted me in the growing crowd, he walked over to us, albeit a little unsteadily. "Donut Hearts should be okay," he said.

"How's Gabby?" I asked him.

His face looked grim. "It's hard to say."

"That was a brave thing you just did going into the fire for her like that," I told him.

The fire chief shrugged off my praise. "It's what I do." He then turned to Jake. "Have you seen Chief Grant anywhere?" Harley asked.

"He's in Union Square," Jake said.

"Well, we need him here," Harley answered, the weariness clear in his words.

"Was it arson?" Jake asked him.

"I can't say for sure one way or the other just yet," Harley admitted. "It's not like that flip of yours that burned down. That was pretty obvious. Whoever did this, if anyone did, was a lot slicker at it." He glanced back at the remnants of the shop. "We got here as fast as we could, but it was too late." Chief Lane seemed remorseful that they hadn't been able to save the place.

"I wouldn't beat myself up about it if I were you. It was already a loss before you even got here," I told him. "I'm just worried about Gabby."

"I am, too," the chief said. "She was breathing when I got to her, but I can't say if she still was when they carted her off. It's a bad night for April Springs, folks."

At that moment, a squad car stopped beside my Jeep, and Chief Grant got out. Stephen Grant had aged quite a bit since taking over the department, and I worried about the effects the job was having on him. Grace, my best friend and his steady, told me that he was finally settling into the role, and I hoped that she was right. I prayed this wouldn't be a setback for him.

"Chief," Stephen said. "Jake. Welcome back, Suzanne," he added as he glanced at me.

"Thanks," I said. "What's going on?"

"I'm coordinating an investigation with Chief Erskine in Union Square. His third day on the job, and somebody started robbing stores in town."

"Not restaurants, I hope," I said, thinking of the DeAngelis clan and their restaurant, Napoli's.

"No, not so far as we know," he admitted. "Anyway, he's asked me for my help, so I've been there all day." Chief Grant turned to the fire chief. "What do you think, Harley?"

"I'm not sure yet. We got a call nine minutes ago," he said. "I was first on the scene and found the back of the building was on fire. I broke the door down in front and found Gabby Williams unconscious in the storeroom. By the time I got there, the front was in flames too, so I busted the back door open and somehow managed to get her out. Don't ask me how I did it, because right now I really couldn't tell you. It's all just one big blur."

"That was nice work, Chief," Grant said.

Again, the older man just shrugged off the compliment. "I was just doing my job." He glanced at Jake. "We've been busier in the past four months than we usually are all year. After the fire at Jake's flip house, I thought things might slow down, but here we are again."

"That was different," Jake protested. "It wasn't even in April Springs, at least not technically."

"I know," Harley said with a sigh. "I'm just saying that some of my new guys are getting more on-the-job experience than I'd like, at least this quickly. They'll be seasoned soon enough. It's even weeded one out."

"What happened?" Jake asked.

"Kenny Dawson was my best recruit. Whenever we had a live drill, he was the first one through the door, and I had high hopes for him."

"Then what?" Chief Grant asked.

"He had his appendix out for your fire, Jake, but he was cleared for duty for this one. He took one look at the fire and got back into his truck and drove away. That guy couldn't get out of here fast enough. I suspect I'll have his resignation on my desk before the night is over."

"And if you don't?" I asked.

"Then I suppose I'll have to fire him," he said with a sigh.

"Can you really even get *fired* from a job you volunteer for?" I followed up.

"When it comes to life and death, you sure can," the chief said. "Anyway, I've got to get back to my people. I'm sure we'll talk later, Chief Grant."

"I'll be here," the chief said as he stared into the flames. The fire was slowly starting to ebb, no doubt in some part because of the constant stream of water still being played out on it.

The police chief was staring into the billowing smoke, and Jake put a hand on his shoulder. "There was nothing you could have done about it even if you'd been here."

"Maybe, maybe not," Chief Grant said woodenly. "Still, I *should* have been here, not in Union Square. This is my town, and it's where I belong."

"First of all, there's nothing that says you could have done anything about this if you were standing in front of the shop when it happened, and second of all, when someone calls you for help, especially the new police chief from another nearby town, you help them if it's within your power to do it." It was a stern lecture from Jake, and I doubted Stephen Grant would have taken it from anyone else, but Jake was a seasoned former law enforcement officer, and he garnered a great deal of respect from his peers.

"Yeah, I know, you're probably right," the chief said softly.

"I realize that you can't let this go, but at least try not to beat yourself up *too* much about it, okay?" Jake asked him.

"I appreciate the sentiment, but in the end, I guess it all depends on how Gabby does," he replied.

Chapter 3

"You've had quite an adventure," Jake said as we cut through the park and headed home. We'd had to move our vehicles all the way over to the parking area of the building my father had left me on Viewmont Avenue, and instead of walking back down Springs Drive, we'd cut across the parking lot behind the jail, the bookstore, and the Boxcar Grill.

"I'm just glad that Autumn is going to be okay," I said as we continued to walk. After we passed the buildings, it was just a short jaunt through the park, and then we were home. We'd have to pick up the Jeep and Jake's truck the next day, but at least my commute wouldn't be a problem. The weather was still nice, and the temperatures remained mostly moderate all through the night.

"Is she really okay?" Jake asked.

"I won't lie to you. It's been rough on her," I said as we walked up onto the porch together, "but I have a feeling that she and Jeff are going to make it."

"That's good to hear. I know how much you care about her," he said as he glanced back at the parking area in front of our cottage. "It looks odd being so empty, doesn't it?"

"I know. I hope Grace manages to get through the barricade, if she's not already home. I need to touch base with her tomorrow. I left town so quickly that I didn't have a chance to bring her up to speed on what I was doing and where I was going."

"I love that you two have been friends for so long," Jake said. "I wish I had that." As he sniffed the air, he added, "The smell from the fire is even here, isn't it?"

"There was a great deal of clothing in that shop," I said. "Most of it was flammable, but clearly at least some of it wasn't." That made me think of Gabby fighting for her life in the hospital. Our lives seemed so normal in that instant, while she was struggling to hold onto hers. It felt odd calling Gabby a friend. The woman could be absolutely caustic at times, but I knew she cared for me, and to my surprise, I'd returned the sentiment. "I wonder how Gabby is doing?"

"You could always call the hospital and find out," Jake suggested.

"They probably won't tell me anything at the front desk, but I know someone who might be willing to open up," I said as I pulled out my phone.

I was in luck. She picked up on the second ring. "Hey, Penny, it's Suzanne." Penny Parsons was a nurse at the hospital, and we'd been friends for years, even if we had gone through some rough patches on occasion.

"Hey. Are you calling about Gabby?"

"I am," I admitted. "How did you know?"

"That seems to be the only time I hear from you lately, when you want something from me," she said a little severely. I'd clearly neglected our friendship lately.

It was time to start doing some damage control. "That's fair. I'm sorry. I have no right to call to ask you anything. Are you free for lunch tomorrow? It's been forever since we did that."

"It has," she agreed a little coolly. "I'm working, though."

"I could treat you to the cafeteria food," I offered.

"Thanks, but since Barton Gleason left to run his own restaurant, we've gone back to the standard bland food we had here before. How's he doing, by the way? Is there any chance his business will fail and he'll come back to us?" Was there an air of hope in her voice as she asked the question?

"Apparently he's doing quite well," I said. Emma had reported to me a few weeks ago that even the chef himself had been surprised by his own success, though one taste of his food would tell even the most common of palates that he was destined for greater things than a hospital cafeteria.

"Good for him," she said, sounding sincere as she said it. "Is he still dating your assistant?"

"He is," I answered. "Tell you what, I'll bring us food from his place, if you'd like."

Penny sighed. "That's all right. I'm sorry I was snippy before. You don't have to bring me anything. I've been working a double shift, and I have to face another one tomorrow. Tell you what. If you're serious about lunch, I'd kill for a cheeseburger from the Boxcar."

"You've got it," I promised. "What time is good for you?"

"Do you still close the donut shop at eleven?" she asked me.

"Unless I sell out early," I answered.

She paused before speaking again. "Has that ever happened?"

"Only on the rarest of occasions," I said, "but I'm ever hopeful."

"Okay, eleven-thirty would be perfect, if you're sure it's not too much trouble."

"It's no trouble at all," I said. "You don't mind me smelling like donuts, do you? I won't have time to go home and shower first."

"Are you kidding? I'd consider that a plus. If you have any extras, I'm sure the nurses would greatly appreciate whatever you're not going to need."

"That's a promise," I said. "I'll see you tomorrow."

I was about to hang up when she said, "Suzanne," softly.

"Yes?"

In a lower voice, she said, "I didn't tell you any of this, but she's not doing great. They're worried about a concussion, and there is some concern about her lungs, too. She's unconscious at the moment, but if I know Gabby, she won't give up without a fight."

"Thanks, I appreciate that," I said somberly. "I'll see you tomorrow."

"What did Penny say?" Jake asked. "Did Gabby die?"

I was lost in my thoughts as I stared at him. "Why do you ask that?"

"The expression on your face," Jake said. "Well?"

"She's still alive, but it doesn't look good," I said.

"I'm sorry," Jake answered, putting an arm around my shoulder. "Are you okay?"

"No, but I will be," I said as I stifled a yawn. "Listen, I hate to poop out on you, but it's been a long day, and tomorrow isn't going to be any easier. I haven't had to get up early for nearly a week."

"Then let's call it a night," he said.

"You don't have to go to sleep just because I'm going to," I told him.

"I'm working with George on the lake house, remember? I'll probably be asleep before you are," he answered with a chuckle.

"I'll take that bet," I said as I headed off to our bedroom.

"There is no way in the world that I'm making that kind of wager with you," he said.

I didn't need the alarm the next morning. As I lay there staring at the clock, waiting for it to go off, I finally decided to go ahead and get up before it woke Jake up. After all, I had to walk to work today since my Jeep was still on the other side of town. I got up quietly, but Jake didn't even stir. The poor guy was still beat, and I wasn't going to rob him of a single minute of sleep if I could help it. I'd become an old pro at getting dressed in the dark, and once I was in the kitchen, I turned on a light that was dimmed low, had a quick bowl of cereal, and then headed out.

I hadn't walked to work in a long time, and as I locked the cottage door behind me, I realized how much I'd missed it. There were sights and sounds at two-thirty in the morning that you couldn't find later in the day. Nearly all of April Springs was still fast asleep, and I liked it that way. I considered walking through the park, but I decided I'd rather take the road instead. There was more light there, and besides, I could go past Grace's place to see if she'd ever made it home.

As predicted, there were no lights on at her home, but her car was in the driveway, so either the road was open again, or she'd been there when the fire had started in the first place. If I didn't hear from her, after my lunch with Penny, I'd call her and bring her up to speed on my life.

There was an eerie white glow in the sky that I hadn't ever seen before, and as I turned the corner and neared my donut shop, I spotted the giant floodlights that had been set up around the rubble that had so recently been an upscale recycled clothing store. As a matter of fact, the lights were so bright that the front of my donut shop was lit up as well. I saw that there were four trucks parked on the street in front of Gabby's place, and I wondered if there was any point in me even making donuts this morning. After all, if my customers couldn't get to me, what good did it do for me to make anything?

I found Chief Grant standing in front of the building that had once housed the now-defunct Patty Cakes Bakery. He was watching a skeleton crew of volunteer firefighters spraying hot spots where Re-NEWed used to be as they sprang up, and every now and then, one of them would shoot some of their spray on the sides of the buildings that housed my donut shop and the former bakery. "How's it going?" I asked him.

"We're just about ready to wrap things up. Give us another ninety minutes and we'll be out of here."

"Did you find what caused the fire yet?" I asked him.

"The fire inspector's still poking around in there," the chief said.

"I don't have anything ready at the moment, but if you give me an hour, I'll have coffee and donuts for you and your team," I offered. "I know how you feel about taking anything for free from the local merchants, but I'd really appreciate it if you'd make an exception this time."

After looking into his eyes, I asked him, "Chief, have you even taken a break since the fire started?"

"No, I've been here the entire time." He pondered my offer, and then he said, "Tell you what. I'll split it with you. If you'll provide the food and drink, I'll cover your costs."

"You've got yourself a deal," I said as I stuck out my hand.

He laughed for a moment as he took it. "Thanks."

"Any word on Gabby?" I asked.

"She's still unconscious, and still in critical condition," he said somberly.

"Thanks for the info. Okay, I'll see you soon," I said as I headed into Donut Hearts.

As I worked, I kept replaying past encounters I'd had with my business neighbor. We'd been through a great deal together, and though she was known for her sharp tongue around town, the two of us had somehow formed a tenuous friendship over the years. With ReNEWed gone and beyond resurrection and the woman herself fighting for her life, I knew that life around my little corner of April Springs would never be the same.

I made extra cake donuts, not only for the law enforcement and fire crews still working next door but for the nurses at the hospital as well. There was no way I was going to risk going there empty-handed.

Since I'd gotten an early start, I was finished with the cake donuts before Emma even made it in. It didn't matter. The dirty pans, bowls, utensils, and other baking tools would be waiting for her whenever she got to the shop. I loaded up the cart we kept in front to collect cups and plates and then headed next door, being careful to lock the shop behind me. I wasn't about to take a chance on allowing anyone to sneak in while I was handing out goodies.

"Wow, that was quick," the chief said the moment he saw me.

"What can I say? Practice makes perfect," I told him. "Should I distribute the coffee and donuts myself, or should I just wait here and hand them out?"

"I don't want to keep you," he said.

I glanced at my watch. "I have a break coming up anyway, so I have some time to spare." I hadn't mixed the yeast donut dough yet, but since I was ahead of schedule, it could wait.

"Thanks," he said as I handed him a cup of coffee and a lemon iced cake donut.

"Are those still your new favorites?" I asked him.

"For the moment," he admitted. He took a healthy sip of coffee and then a substantial bite of donut. "That's amazing. There's nothing like a hot donut fresh out of the glaze, is there?"

"One chain has made its living off them," I admitted, "but my customers rarely get to sample them quite so fresh."

"That reminds me," he said as he put his paper cup down on the cart and retrieved his wallet. "What do I owe you?"

"Twenty bucks should cover it," I said.

One eyebrow arched as he scanned the cart, which was loaded down with donuts, not to mention the large urn of coffee. "Suzanne."

I lowered my voice. "My profit margins are pretty good, but if you tell anybody I said that, I'll call you a liar to your face," I said with a grin.

"This may cover your supplies, but we both know you have a lot of bills that aren't covered in that twenty."

"I was opening the shop anyway," I said, "so it's not like this is costing me much in heating and electricity."

"Those cups and plates have to cost at least twenty bucks all by themselves."

"Look at them closer," I said with a grin. "Is it anywhere *close* to Christmas right now?"

"No," he admitted.

"I bought them at Cheap Cheeps in Union Square," I admitted. "They practically paid me to take them."

"I love that place," he admitted. "Okay, I appreciate you doing this."

"It is my pleasure," I said as some of the workers started noticing what we were up to. "Come and get it while it's hot," I called out to them.

The hose went off and headed to the ground in an instant, and the officers patrolling the perimeter joined us as well. Before I knew it, they nearly wiped out everything I'd brought. "Wow, that was like a horde of locusts," I said with a grin after they'd all fueled up.

"They clearly love your treats," the chief said as he finished his second donut, a blueberry cake that he'd managed to snag before they were all gone.

"It doesn't hurt that they were all starving," I said as I looked around. "Where's Harley?"

"The fire chief is at the hospital," Chief Grant said.

"Is he okay?" I asked. I couldn't bear the thought of him being hurt, too.

"He wrenched his back carrying Gabby out of the building," the chief said softly. "He wouldn't go get it looked at until one of his guys finally forced him into his truck practically at gunpoint. He's not a young man anymore."

"You'd never know it by the way he saved Gabby," I said.

"It's crazy what you can do when the adrenaline's flowing," the chief said. "Thanks for doing this. Are you sure I can't give you a little more cash?"

"We're good," I said.

I wheeled my empty cart back to Donut Hearts just in time to see Emma unlocking the front door. "I wasn't sure we'd be open," Emma said.

"And yet you came in anyway," I answered with a grin. I saw someone in the shadows behind her, and in a soft voice, I said, "Emma, don't turn around, but someone's following you."

"It's Dad," she said softly. Ray Blake and I had nearly come to blows before I'd left to see Autumn, and the man had every right to be gunshy around me. It didn't help that somehow my history of investigating murder had preceded me when I'd gotten to Autumn's place, all courtesy of Ray's newspaper stories in the past hinting about my involvement in solving crimes in the past.

"He's afraid of you."

"Really? Your father is smarter than he looks," I said loudly. After what had just happened to Gabby, I was in no mood to deal with him at the moment. "Are you ready to get to work?" I asked her as she held the door for me and I wheeled the cart inside.

"Ready, willing, able, and raring to go," she said. "Welcome back. How's your old roommate?"

"Don't call her old to her face." I grinned for a moment. "She's doing okay. Thanks for asking," I said, not really wanting to get into it with Emma. I was in the mood to make more donuts, which was a good thing, because that was what was on my to-do list next.

Chapter 4

"It's crazy what happened to Gabby, isn't it?" Paige Hill asked me a little after nine. Elfin in appearance, Paige's wispy blond hair was stylishly done up with old-fashioned typewriter key–faced barrettes. I'd been getting a steady stream of customers wanting the inside scoop about ReNEWed burning to the ground, but so far, there wasn't anything new to report. As far as I knew, Gabby was still unconscious, and the fire inspector hadn't reported his findings to the police, at least as far as I knew. Of course, Chief Grant was under no obligation to tell me anything.

I just liked it better when he shared with me.

"It is," I admitted as I boxed up a dozen donuts for The Last Page. "What's your book group discussing today? I'm not even sure which one is meeting."

"It's the SFC today," she said.

"The SF probably stands for science fiction, but what about the C?"

"It stands for classics," she said. "They're doing one of Robert Heinlein's books this morning."

"Like *Glory Road*? I loved reading that book when I was a teenager," I admitted. I'd mostly devoured mysteries in my youth, but I'd ventured into the world of science fiction as well on occasion, and there weren't many more traditional than Heinlein in my eyes. "Or are they doing *Stranger in a Strange Land*? That's what he seems to be mostly remembered for these days."

"As a matter of fact, they're discussing *A Door Into Summer*," she said. "Have you read it?"

"Yes, I'm a huge fan of that one, too."

"You should come over and join the group," Paige said. "I'm sure they wouldn't mind."

I didn't even have to think about it. "I'd better not. Thanks for the offer, but things are a little crazy here at the moment."

Paige shrugged. "When *aren't* they, Suzanne? Come on, I know you miss your group. Have you heard from any of the ladies recently?"

I shrugged. "I get emails from them every now and then," I admitted. "After the festival, I was hoping that we'd start right back up where we left off, but we can't seem to get it going again. Maybe our book club's time has just passed us by."

"Don't let that happen," Paige insisted. "Why don't *you* push them into coming back? If you don't want to hold it here, you could always do it at my shop."

"Thanks," I said. "I'll think about it."

"If you decide to try again, I've got just the traditional mystery series for you. Have you ever done a Carolyn Hart novel? I just reread *Death on Demand* for the seventh time, and I've got to tell you, it gets better every time I read it. Also, I've heard that she's a delightful lady in real life, which is always an added bonus in my book. Anyway, *I* really enjoyed it." She paused a moment and then asked, "I never thought about it before, but are you two related, by any chance?"

"I don't know, but I'd like to think there's some distant connection. I admire her work greatly. I've read that book, and I loved it too, but it's been a while. I'll have to think about it," I said.

Lowering her voice, she asked, "How's Gabby doing? I've been asking around, but nobody seems to know anything."

"Same here. I'm going by the hospital after I close Donut Hearts," I admitted. "Maybe I'll be able to get a little more info then."

"If you do, let me know, okay? We all need to stick together," Paige said.

"I will."

I figured our conversation was finished, but then I realized that there was obviously something still on Paige's mind. "Was there anything else?" I asked her.

"No, never mind," she said after a moment or two of hesitation.

"Paige, what is it?"

"I've just spent the last few hours wondering why someone would want to burn Gabby out," she said in an even more subdued voice.

"Does that mean that you don't think it was an accident?" I asked her softly.

"I suppose it could be, but I can't help but wonder."

"About?" I asked her.

"Suzanne, a few days ago, I was taking a walk around town, following the old abandoned railroad tracks, and on my way back to the bookstore, I glanced over at the backs of Donut Hearts, ReNEWed, and Patty Cakes."

"We all share a parking area back there," I said. "What about it?"

"There's more than that. It was hard for me to figure out which building was which if I hadn't already known. There's no real signage on any of the buildings in the back."

"What's your point?" I asked her.

"Can we be absolutely certain that if someone torched ReNEWed, they weren't really trying to set fire to your place instead?"

I must have reacted oddly as I took that in, because Paige quickly added, "Forget I said anything. I've been reading too many mysteries lately. I'm sure it's just my overactive imagination. We're going to find out in a few hours that it was a bad circuit, or someone flipped a cigarette butt into the trash can, or something like that, and it can all be explained away."

"Probably," I said, chewing over the idea that the arson had been meant for me and not Gabby. It was a chilling thought that I hadn't even considered up until that point.

"I'm sorry I said anything. I know I've upset you," she said.

"No, it's fine. I'm good," I said, and then I tapped the box of donuts she'd already paid for. "Not that I don't love having you around, but shouldn't you be getting back to the bookstore? You don't want to keep your book club waiting."

"You're right," she said as she picked the box up. "Suzanne, are we good?"

"Good as gold," I said with a smile.

"Okay. Let me know about Gabby later, okay?"

"You bet," I said.

After Paige was gone, I started chewing over what she'd said. It was true that it had been difficult to tell from the backs of our shops which business was which, but that didn't necessarily mean that an arsonist had mistaken Gabby's shop for mine. Then again, since Patty Cakes had stood empty for some time, there certainly hadn't been any reason to burn that building to the ground. I was going to have to get the official verdict on the reason for Gabby's fire. Otherwise I'd be looking over my shoulder and wondering who might be out to get me for a very long time.

"Hey, Grace," I said as my best friend walked into the shop. "I was going to stop by and see you later. What are you doing in town?"

"Catching up on paperwork, as always," she answered. Grace was stylish and petite, while I was constantly twelve pounds overweight. Why did I seem to have so many diminutive friends? Then again, none of them worked in a donut shop, so who knew how heavy they might be if they faced the temptations I did on a daily basis? "Have you found anything out about Gabby?"

"No, but I'm meeting Penny at the hospital for lunch, so while I'm there, I'll ask around," I said softly. I had half a dozen customers nursing their coffees, their donuts long ago consumed. I had to wonder how many of them were sticking around just in case I said something interesting about what had happened next door.

"She's a good source to have," Grace agreed.

"That's *not* why I'm taking her lunch," I answered softly. "She called me on something, and she was absolutely right. I've been letting down my end of our friendship lately, so this is going to be a strictly social call. As a matter of fact, I'm grabbing us a couple of burgers from the Boxcar Grill and taking them to the hospital after I close the shop, but I'm not bringing up Gabby's name, at least not with her." I had a sudden thought. "Hey, would you like to join us? It could be fun."

"I'd love to, but I've got a hard deadline of twelve noon to get these reports in, so I'll have to pass." She hesitated and then added, "I'll be free later if you want to do something."

"Sounds good," I said. "Jake is tied up with this remodel with George, so he'll be busy all afternoon."

"That suits me," she said. "I don't mind being second choice."

She was clearly joking, but was there a hint of steel in her voice below the surface? I took her hands in mine. "You have *never* been my second choice for *anything*, and you never will be. I can't imagine my life without you in it."

She squeezed my hands before letting go. "Suzanne, lighten up. I was just kidding," she answered with a grin.

"Okay, if you're sure," I said. Penny already felt that I hadn't been the best friend to her that I could be, and I didn't want Grace to feel that way, too.

"Absolutely positive," she said with a smile. "But if buying me dinner tonight will make you feel better, I won't say no."

"We'll see," I said with a grin of my own. "Now go do that paperwork."

"Yes, ma'am," she said, saluting me and then leaving Donut Hearts to finish up her reports. I suddenly realized that Grace hadn't ordered anything. That was when I knew that she'd been there to check up on me, to make sure that I was handling what had happened next door well. It was just one of the things that made her such a good friend, and I was once again—and always—thankful that she was in my life.

"Hey, Momma. What are you doing here?"

My mother, yet another petite woman in my life, looked a bit frazzled, which was unusual for her. Usually she was the type of person who gave other folks ulcers, but she was clearly being tested at the moment. It was fifteen minutes before I was due to close, and I was already preparing to shut the place down for another day. "How's Phillip doing?"

"As a matter of fact, he seems to be getting crankier by the minute," she said as she bit her lower lip.

"He's probably in pain," I allowed.

"No doubt, and the stubborn old fool won't take the drugs his doctors have prescribed for him. The only thing he'll take is something over the counter that's more suited for a headache or a hangnail than for what he's going through."

"Why is he resisting?" I asked.

"He's afraid he'll get addicted after one or two pills," she said. "As much as I've tried to convince him otherwise, he won't listen to me."

"So you had to get out of the house for a few minutes?" I asked her sympathetically. "I'm honored that you chose to come here with your limited amount of free time."

Momma looked a bit guilty as she admitted, "Suzanne, I do love seeing you, but I have an ulterior motive."

"I'd love to help you take care of him," I said. "Things are just a little crazy right now, but I should be free by this evening."

Momma took my hands in hers. "Darling child, I would never dream of asking you to do that. No, Phillip has been requesting an apple fritter, a lemon-filled donut, and a plain glazed one. Please tell me you still have one of each in stock."

"And you're going to give him all three?" I asked, astounded by the news. Phillip had lost a great deal of weight in his efforts to court my mother, but lately she'd been helping watch his calorie intake so he didn't revert to his old ways.

"I am," she admitted. "Don't judge me, Suzanne."

"I wouldn't dream of it," I said as I bagged up the treats, which I fortuitously had on hand. "May I throw something in for you as well?"

"I could probably use a sugar rush to help me cope with him, but I'll pass."

"Some coffee, perhaps?" I suggested.

"That I will take," she said as she reached for her purse.

"If you finish that motion, you and I are going to have a problem," I said with a smile.

Momma moved her hand away instantly. "Believe me, having a problem with one family member at the moment is more than enough for me."

"How's he feeling, really?" I asked her as I handed her the coffee and the treats.

"He's feeling his age, which is never a good thing," Momma said sympathetically. "I'm sure he'll be fine, but it's going to take some time."

"I wouldn't want anyone else taking care of me but you, if I were him," I said gently. "You are amazing."

Momma began to tear up for a moment, but then she quickly got her emotions under control again. "That's *exactly* what I needed to hear," she said. "I'm so happy you're mine."

"Right back at you," I said.

Almost as an afterthought, Momma asked, "Is there any news on Gabby?"

"The last I heard, there was no change," I admitted.

"I know she presents a crusty exterior to the world, but she's got a good heart, and she thinks the world of you, Suzanne."

"I appreciate that," I told her. "I just wish there was something I could do to help her."

"Just be there for her when she needs you, as you are for me," Momma answered.

"There doesn't seem to be much else that I can do," I admitted.

"You'd be surprised by how much of an impact you have on the lives of the people around you," Momma said, and then she took off, no doubt to get home to her husband and help him recover, not just his health but his generally positive attitude as well. I'd have to see if I could come up with something to help lift his spirits, but for the moment, I had other things on my mind.

In fact, I was still mulling over my next move when I saw Chief Grant approach the donut shop two minutes before I was set to close Donut Hearts for the day.

Maybe I'd finally get some answers to the questions that were swirling around in my head.

Chapter 5

"**I** really appreciate you taking care of all of us this morning," the chief said.

"Hey, you paid for it," I said as I continued wiping down the counter. "Can I get you something while you're here?" I had plenty of donuts left over for Penny, but I could certainly spare a few for the police chief.

"No thanks, I'm good," he said. He looked around at my empty shop and then gestured toward the kitchen. "Is Emma still back there?"

"At the moment, she has her earbuds cranked up, and she's rocking to something while she does dishes. For all intents and purposes, I'm alone."

He nodded, but I noticed that he still kept his voice down. "There are a few things I wanted to talk to you about."

"Go on," I said. "Do I need to stop working while you talk?"

"No, go ahead and do whatever it is you need to do," he answered.

"Good enough," I said as I locked us in and flipped the sign to CLOSED. "What's up?"

"The SBI fire and arson investigator just left," he said. "I thought you might want to know what he found."

"Was the fire at ReNEWed intentionally set?" I asked as I stopped sweeping for a second.

"No, it appears Gabby's toaster oven in back had a short in the cord and caught some nearby boxes of clothes on fire. He didn't have his dog with him, but he was pretty sure that was what caused it."

"What does his dog have to do with anything?" I asked. "Is that new?"

"No, the SBI has been using trained dogs since the mid-eighties," he said. "They can smell accelerants down to the smallest trace, but this guy's dog has a head cold, of all things, so he stayed home. Anyway, he found the frayed cord and the boxes at the heart of where the fire started, so he was pretty confident in saying that it was accidental and not natural or intentional."

"If that's the case, then what happened to Gabby?"

The chief shrugged. "We'll probably have to wait for her to tell us, but my guess is that sometime between six and seven p.m., she spotted the fire, panicked, tried to put it out, and slipped on something and fell in the process. Either that, or the smoke overcame her and she passed out. Whichever scenario is true, she must have hit her head as she fell. It's the only way it makes sense."

"I can think of some other possibilities," I said as I resumed sweeping.

"Suzanne, not *everything* that happens around here is due to a criminal act."

"I know that," I answered, "but that doesn't mean that it's all innocent, either."

"I agree, but there's really not much we can do until Gabby regains consciousness."

"But," I said.

"But what?"

"There was definitely a 'but' hanging in the air just then. You were going to say *if* she recovers, weren't you?"

Chief Grant frowned a moment before answering. "Well, the truth of the matter is that she's been out for a while."

"What do the doctors have to say?" I asked.

"I haven't spoken with them in the past few hours. I've been with the SBI guy next door."

"Did he happen to know Jake, by any chance?" I asked. "My husband still has a great many friends with the State Bureau of Investigation."

"I asked him, but he's pretty new. He didn't know him. I asked Jake about it, and he didn't know the guy, either, so there you go."

"When did you talk to Jake?" I asked him, more out of curiosity than anything else.

The police chief immediately looked guilty. "Maybe you should ask him about that yourself."

"I will, but he's not here right now, and you are," I said with a smile. "Come on, Stephen. We've known each other for a long time. What's going on?"

The police chief shrugged, and after letting out a long sigh, he said, "I've been talking to him about the robberies in Union Square this morning."

"There were more robberies *today*?" I asked him. What was happening in that quaint little sister city of ours?

"That's not what I meant. I should have said that I spoke with Jake this morning about what's going on in Union Square."

"I didn't think you were going to get involved anymore."

"I'm not, at least not as much as Chief Erskine would like me to. He wants me to team up with him on the case, but I've got my hands full dealing with April Springs at the moment. I suggested to him that he might want to reach out to Jake and hire him as a consultant. I'm sorry for not running it by you first," he added, "but I thought Jake would be perfect for the job."

"You know what? He would be," I said, realizing that it was true. "Is he taking it?"

"He said that he wasn't interested, that he wasn't a cop anymore, and that he wanted to leave it to the professionals," the chief admitted.

"Did you believe he meant any part of that?" I asked him gently.

"Like I said, maybe you should discuss it with him," the chief said reluctantly.

"Okay, I'll do that," I said. "Thanks for thinking of him, Chief."

"Hey, I should have thought of him before and suggested it in the first place," Chief Grant said with a smile. "We both know that Jake is the best cop in a five-hundred-mile radius."

"Used to be, you mean," I corrected him.

"He still is, in my opinion. Those skills don't go away just because you hand in your badge." The chief shrugged. "Anyway, I thought you might want to know what they found at the scene next door. You don't have anything to worry about."

I thought about sharing Paige's idea with him that ReNEWed might not have been the target after all, but given what the police chief had told me, I decided to keep that speculation to myself. "And you believe it's true?"

"Which part of it?" he asked me with a frown.

"*All* of it," I answered. "What you're saying is that the official verdict of the state of North Carolina is that the fire was accidental, and so was Gabby's injury. Is that right?"

"Yes, that's the way things stand at the moment, unless we learn something that counters that. Why do you want to know?"

"It's easy. If *you* don't believe there was a crime committed next door, then you won't mind if Grace and I do a little digging on our own, would you?" I asked him with a grin.

Chief Grant let out a long sigh before he answered. "I don't suppose there's anything I can do about it, is there? Go on. Knock yourself out."

"Thanks, that's exactly what I was hoping you'd say."

"Suzanne, do you know something that I don't?" The question was sincere. The police chief really wanted my opinion on the matter. It was a far cry from the way my stepfather had behaved when I'd first started investigating homicides on my own.

"The truth of the matter is that I find it hard to believe that Gabby slipped and fell—whether from the smoke or from the excitement—and it's almost as likely that she would *never* use a toaster oven in her shop."

"Why wouldn't she?"

"If something she was toasting happened to burn, which things sometimes do in toaster ovens, the smell could easily get into the clothes, and that would reduce their value greatly, or else she'd have to pay to have everything cleaned again. In all of the years I've known her, I've *never* seen her use anything like that in her shop, and I've spent quite a bit of time in the back with her, too."

"I can understand what you're saying, but there's really no hard evidence to back all of this speculation up, is there?"

"Not yet, at least," I said with a grin.

The police chief headed for the door, and after I unlocked it and let him out, he turned back and looked at me before I closed it again. "Suzanne, if you do happen to stumble across anything, keep me posted, okay?"

"You bet," I said. "Thanks for coming by."

"Happy to do it. All a part of the service, ma'am," he added with a grin as he tipped his imaginary cap to me and then left.

Once he was gone and Emma and I were safely locked inside again, I had to wonder if maybe the inspector—and the chief—were right after all. Were Grace and I investigating something that had really just been an unfortunate accident? Or had it just been staged to look that way?

Until Gabby could tell us what had really happened, we were going to go forward with the case.

I wasn't about to let an attempt on my friend's life go unpunished, especially if it turned out to be a successful one.

"Hey, Trish, it's Suzanne," I said when I finally got the owner of the Boxcar Grill on the phone. "Things must be hopping there."

"It's crazy," she admitted. "I know you're not calling ahead for a reservation, so what can I do for you?"

"Since when did you start taking reservations?" I asked her. The diner was strictly casual dining, and though it got busy at times, I couldn't imagine anyone trying to reserve a table.

"I don't, at least not for the general public, but I'm always willing to make an exception for you."

I took a deep breath and asked a question that I knew was going to get me in trouble with my friend. Trish believed food should be eaten as soon after it had been prepared as possible, and I generally agreed with her, but I couldn't bring Penny to the diner, so I was going to have to make a special request. "Listen, I hate to ask, but I'm trying to patch things up with Penny Parsons, and I promised her I'd bring her a cheeseburger from the Boxcar. Is there any chance you'd bag a couple up for me? I wouldn't ask if it weren't important."

"Like I said, for you, I'll do it. Anything else? Please tell me you're not ordering French fries. The burgers travel okay, but the fries absolutely do not."

"Just a pair of teas to go with them is all I want," I assured her. "Thanks. You're a real lifesaver."

"Don't you know it," she said, and I could hear the smile in her voice. "Suzanne, what did you do to Penny?"

"It appears that I've been taking her for granted lately," I admitted.

"Does that mean that *I'll* be getting lunch with you sometime soon, too?" she asked me.

"I'm sorry. I didn't mean to take you for granted, too. Can you ever forgive me?" It wasn't like me to turn my back on my friends, but I must have been so wrapped up with my family and Autumn lately that

I hadn't budgeted enough time for the people I cared about, which was something I was going to correct as soon as possible.

"Hey, it's no big deal. I just miss hanging out with you," she said.

"I miss you, too. How can I make it up to you?"

"Bring Grace with you tomorrow to the Boxcar if you can make it, and we can catch up and have a feast here. How does that sound?"

"If it's humanly possible, I'll be there, and if Grace can get free, I know she'd love to see you, too."

"That's all a girl can ask for then," she said. "I'll have your burgers and drinks ready by the time you walk over here. By the way, any word on Gabby?"

"Not that I've heard," I admitted. "See you in a minute."

"I'll be here," she said.

I turned to find my assistant listening to the conversation. "You and I already spend plenty of time together," she said with a grin, "not that I'd mind you buying me lunch someday, too."

I laughed. "I figured you'd be sick of seeing me after working with me all morning," I said. "Do me a favor, would you?"

"Anything," she said. "All you have to do is ask."

"You'd better be careful making an open-ended offer like that. I just need you to run our deposit by the bank when you leave here. I've got a few errands to run."

"I heard," she said with a smile. "While you're picking up your lunch supplies for you and Penny, I can load the extra donuts in the back of your Jeep."

"That would be great," I said. "They're going to the nurses station that's closest to Gabby."

As I headed for the door, Emma said, "That's a really sweet thing to do. I'm not sure, but I have a feeling that you're one of her closest friends. How did you ever get past that gruff exterior of hers?"

"I don't know. I'll let you know if I ever do," I said with a wry smile. "Trust me, it surprises me as much as it does everyone else in town that

Gabby and I have become friends over the years. I'd hate to lose her." The thought chilled me as I voiced it. It was true enough. If Gabby didn't pull through this, I'd miss having her in my life. If she *did* manage to survive whatever had really happened to her, I was going to tell her how I felt about her, no matter how uncomfortable it might make both of us feel.

I just hoped I got the chance.

Chapter 6

"Does this sudden lunch at the hospital have anything to do with Gabby?" Trish asked me softly as I handed her the money for my take-out order.

"While I'm there, I'll probably ask around about her, but no, it's mostly for Penny."

"You're a good friend, Suzanne, and we're all lucky to have you in our lives."

"I feel the same way about you," I started to say when she interrupted me.

"Hang on. I wasn't finished. Don't pay the slightest bit of attention to what I'm about to say." In a louder voice, she added, "This is the last time I'm letting you order food to go. I don't like it, and what's more, you know it. Do you understand?" As she scolded me, her back was turned to the dining room, and she added a wink at the end of her little speech to let me know that this outburst was for everyone else's benefit, not mine.

"I'm sorry. I won't let it happen again," I said, sounding appropriately remorseful, or at least trying to.

"See to it," she said as she smiled, and then, in a softer voice, she said, "I'll see you tomorrow."

"Not if I see you first," I added, doing everything in my power not to match her smile. "Thanks for this," I whispered.

"Anytime, for you," she said. "If you see Gabby, tell her I said hello."

"If I see her, and she's awake, I will."

"It's bad, isn't it?" Trish asked me.

"It's not good," I admitted. "Listen, you didn't happen to spot anything unusual going on at ReNEWed over the last few days, have you?"

She started to answer, "Maybe. I thought I saw..." but then Nathan from the sporting goods store approached with his bill, and she shut the sentence off instantly.

"Suzanne, you're playing with fire, girl. I can't believe you had the nerve to order something to go, no matter how good friends you two are. I shouldn't have to tell you that you don't want to make Trish's naughty list," Nathan said with a grin.

"Neither do you, Nathan," Trish said, barely smiling back.

The shop owner looked appropriately chastised. "No, ma'am, I do not." Nathan pointed to my bag of cheeseburgers. "If you're going to eat those, you'd better get going."

"You're right," I said, reluctant to leave the Boxcar Grill until Trish could tell me what she'd been about to say before we'd been interrupted. "We'll talk later?" I asked her as I headed for the door.

"You bet," Trish said. She looked a bit troubled as I walked out. I had to wonder what she had been about to tell me. Had it been something important, or had it just taken on significance only *after* the gently used clothing shop had burned to the ground? I'd have to ask her later, but it was going to have to wait for now.

Nathan was right about one thing. I needed to get those burgers to the hospital so Penny and I could enjoy them while they were hot. After we ate and I delivered the donuts, I'd make my way to Gabby and check on how she was doing.

I hoped she was finally awake, because as every minute slipped by that she was still unconscious, my concern for her grew stronger.

"Dinner is served," I told Penny as I delivered the cheeseburgers and iced tea to the outside table where she was waiting for me in front of the hospital. I hadn't even had a chance to get into the building when I'd heard her calling my name.

"Are you sure you don't mind eating outside? It's such a beautiful day, isn't it?"

"Gorgeous," I said. "How's your day been so far?"

"As far as I'm concerned, working in the hospital is tougher than being in a doctor's office, and it doesn't always necessarily pay any better, but it's more exciting and fast paced, at least for me. How about you? How's your day?"

"What can I say? I get up, I make donuts, I sell donuts, I go home, and then I start all over again the next day," I said with a grin.

"Don't lie to me. You love it," Penny said as she took her first bite. "This is amazing."

"I'll let Trish know. As a matter of fact, I do enjoy what I do," I admitted. After taking a bite of my own burger, I added, "I have no idea why Trish is so opposed to take-out. This is delightful."

"She cares about what she does just as much as we do, and she wants folks to experience the very best she has to offer. You don't sell donuts that are three days old, do you?"

"Are you kidding? I donate ones I don't move the same day I make them if they don't sell," I admitted. "Not that I'm doing that to you. I've got six dozen fresh donuts in the back of my Jeep, and as soon as we finish eating, we can deliver them to the nurses stations around the hospital."

"That sounds wonderful. I know they'll love them. Thanks for thinking of us."

"You bet," I said. "How are things going otherwise with you?"

"Do you mean my love life?" she asked.

"I do."

"It's not going anywhere at all, truth be told, but I don't mind. I've got a lot going on at the moment, and a man would just get in the way."

She looked at me a moment longer, and then she burst out laughing. "Okay, I wouldn't mind one coming around every now and then."

"Penny, you're too good not to have someone in your life if that's what you want," I told her.

"That's what I think, too," she answered with a grin. "How's Jake doing these days?"

"He's currently helping the mayor remodel his lake house, and the two of them are having a ball doing it."

"I'm sure they are," she said as she took another bite.

After Penny finished eating, she leaned back and enjoyed a bit of sunshine. "I love this," she said.

"My company, or the picnic lunch?" I asked her.

"Is there any reason that it can't be both?" Penny asked with a chuckle, never opening her eyes. After a few moments, she sat back up. "If you're finished eating too, let's grab those donuts. Are you sure I can't give you anything for them?"

"I'm positive," I said as I took our trash and threw everything away in a nearby can. "Let's play Santa Claus and start delivering our goodies."

"It sounds like a blast to me," she said.

After we delivered donuts to every station and also a box to two of the lounges, I gave Penny a hug. "I'm glad we could do this," I said.

"So am I," she said. "I'm proud of you, Suzanne."

"Why? Not that I don't love hearing it," I answered.

"You didn't ask about Gabby even once during the entire meal and our deliveries."

"This lunch was about us, not her," I said. I'd been tempted to ask her a few times during our meal, but I'd managed to restrain myself, and now I was glad that I had.

"Well, I have a few more minutes before I have to go back to work. Let's talk about her now."

"Are you sure?" I asked her.

"I'm positive. As a matter of fact, I've got something you might want to hear."

"Go on, I'm listening," I said, eager to hear what she had to say.

"Gabby came out of it for just a few seconds, and I happened to be nearby when she did," Penny admitted.

"Really? Did she happen to say anything?"

"She was clearly still out of it, but I think I heard her say 'fire.' I couldn't be sure, and by the time I bent down closer to her to hear better, she was out of it again." Penny frowned. "It's really no surprise, given what happened to her."

"No, it's not," I said, a little dashed by the revelation. If I'd been in my shop and it happened to be engulfed in flames at the time, I'm sure the fire would be foremost in my thoughts.

"Gabby had just gone through a pretty traumatic experience, and her voice was barely above a whisper. She could have been trying to say any number of other things. Sorry it's not more encouraging than that."

"I appreciate you sharing it with me," I said sincerely. "How's she doing? Really?"

"Gabby's official status is still critical," Penny said carefully.

"I understand that, but what do you think her odds are of getting through this alive?"

Penny shrugged and considered the question before answering. "I'll deny it if you tell anyone I said it, but at this point I'd say it's a coin toss. I'm sorry, I know the two of you are friends, but you deserve to know the truth."

"That means more to me than I can say," I said as I hugged her. "Thanks for being honest with me about it." I wanted to ask her to keep me updated on Gabby's condition, but given the fact that I was there in order to mend bridges with her, I decided it wasn't the right thing to do.

"Listen, if anything changes, I'll give you a call," she volunteered.

"I'd appreciate that, but you don't have to do that. That's really not why I came." In the spirit of being candid, I added, "Well, not entirely. I was going to check on her after lunch, but I wasn't going to ask you to keep an eye on her for me."

"You didn't ask; I volunteered," Penny said with a smile. "Lunch was great, and I know everyone will appreciate the donuts, but I've got to get back to work."

"Thanks for making the time for me," I said. "I'll try to be a better friend."

"You're doing just fine," Penny answered, and then she hurried to make it back to her station in time to get to work.

It was just as well. I had a great deal to do myself. First of all, I had to go back and pick Grace up, and then we needed to go talk to Trish. She'd clearly seen something that had troubled her going on at Re-NEWed, and I was determined to find out what it was.

"How was lunch?" Grace asked me after letting me into her place. It was as neat as could be, all except for her dining room table. That was covered with stacks of paper that went several layers deep, and there was a shredder stationed right beside it.

"It was good," I said as I looked around. "Listen, if this is a bad time for you, we don't have to do this right now."

Grace waved a hand toward the table. "This? Don't be fooled by the stacks. I have to do this once a quarter. We used to keep all of these reports on hand for years, but my new boss is trying to get us to go paperless, which would be fine with me if some of my staff actually knew how to use their computers. I thought the kids these days were raised on them."

It sounded funny hearing her refer to her employees as kids, but then I realized that most of them were probably a good ten years younger than we were. "I'm willing to bet that's true on a case-by-case basis only," I said. "What are the paper mills going to do without your business if you ever manage to do away with it completely?" I asked her with a grin.

"Oh, I'm pretty sure they'll be okay. The transition is going to take a while, and in the meantime, we're doing our paperwork *both* ways."

"Electronically *and* physically?" I asked her. "That seems like a lot of unnecessary work to me."

"You don't have to tell me that, but if I don't reconcile the reports, I get two different answers to the same question from some of my people. No worries; I've got a system. The second I manage to get everything squared away, I shred the paper and keep the electronic file."

"How often do the totals disagree?" I asked her. I'd never worked in an office, let alone for a corporation as large as the one Grace worked for, and it amazed me at times how much energy and effort they spent just communicating with each other. If I had something going on at work, I either told Emma directly, or I left her a note. Then again, I was sure it was a lot easier when only two people were involved instead of dozens and dozens spread out up and down the corporate ladder.

"That's where those boxes come into play," she said as she pointed to a stack of packing boxes just off the living room. She must have seen my surprised reaction, because she quickly added, "They aren't full, so don't look so stunned. Right now I have about thirty reports left to reconcile. These all get shredded."

"Do you want some help?" I asked her. "That sounds like it could be fun."

"You *enjoy* shredding documents?" she asked me incredulously.

"Hey, I look at it as making confetti that no one will ever throw," I said. "What's not to love? We can take half an hour and knock it out if we work together." I was eager to investigate what had happened at ReNEWed, but I knew that Grace had her own set of obligations, so if I could help her with some of those, she'd be free to help me do a little digging.

"I'd appreciate that," she said. "Go for it."

As I flipped the massive shredder on, I asked, "Is there anything I have to watch out for?"

"No, this thing eats staples and paperclips like snacks. Chuck them in the chute ten or twelve sheets at a time and you should be fine."

"I can do that," I said as I started feeding in the reports and reducing them to scrap paper. That shredder was industrial strength for sure. Not only did it handle metal, but it shredded everything horizontally *and* vertically. There was something hypnotizing about watching the paperwork disappear, and I found myself caught up in the rhythm of the cutters.

After I finished clearing the table, leaving the top completely paperless, I asked her, "Is there anything else I can shred?"

"You really *do* enjoy that, don't you?" she asked me with a smile. "Sorry, but that's it for now. The rest I have to go through later, but you've been a big help."

"It was nothing," I said. "Are you sure you have time to help me?"

"I've got plenty of time now," she said.

"What about those reports you still have to reconcile? I don't want to pull you away if you need to work."

"Suzanne, I've got to have *something* to do tomorrow while you're making donuts, don't I?" she asked me with a grin. "Come on. Let's go."

"All right," I said.

Grace hesitated a moment. "Where exactly do we start?"

"That one's easy. I was talking to Trish earlier, and I think she may have seen something at ReNEWed yesterday," I said.

"Before the fire?"

"That's my theory, but there's only one way to find out."

"Then let's go have a chat with her," Grace said. "While we're there, I can grab something to eat."

"I'm sorry. I didn't even think about *your* lunch."

"Hey, I'm a big girl. I eat when I get hungry," she said. "Besides, you don't mind keeping me company while I have myself a feast, do you?"

"Not at all. In fact, I may even have a piece of pie, just to keep you company, you understand."

Grace grinned at me. "You always were the politest person I knew."

"Liar," I answered with a smile of my own.

"Hey, if you're having pie, then I'll have some for dessert myself. Let's go."

Once we were outside, I asked, "Why don't we walk over to the Boxcar? Once we decide what to do next, we can come back for my Jeep, but for now, I can work up an appetite for that pie."

"That sounds good to me," she said.

As we headed up Springs Drive on foot, I found myself hesitating at the donut shop before we followed the long defunct railroad tracks in the opposite direction toward the Boxcar Grill. The remains of Gabby's shop beside mine were a reminder of just how close I'd come to losing everything myself. The hole between Donut Hearts and the old Patty Cakes building was like a missing tooth. The place had burned rather thoroughly, and I had to wonder how long it would be until the remains were bulldozed and hauled away. In six months, would anyone even be able to tell that Gabby's shop had once stood there so proudly? It always amazed me how tenuous civilization was and how quickly nature reclaimed her own space.

"Hey, are you okay?" Grace asked as she touched my shoulder lightly.

"I'm fine," I said as I shook myself slightly. "I think someone must have just walked over my grave."

Grace shivered. "I always hated that expression."

"Me, too," I agreed. "Come on. Let's go get you something to eat."

Chapter 7

"How was your lunch, Suzanne?" Trish asked me critically the moment she spied me coming into the diner. "Tell me the truth. It was cold by the time you ate it, wasn't it?"

"As a matter of fact, it was delightful," I told her. "Penny told me to tell you thanks for making an exception for us. She said it was exactly what she needed to get her through the rest of her day."

That seemed to mollify her slightly. "Okay, I'll be sure to thank her for the kind words the next time I see her," she said. "What's up?"

"I was hoping to get a bite to eat myself," Grace said.

"Are you going to try to take it with you?" Trish asked her pointedly.

"No, ma'am, not on your life. I'll have the meat loaf special and an iced tea, for here."

Trish grinned. "That's what I'm talking about. Go grab a table, and I'll bring it out to you." Almost as an afterthought, she turned back to me. "Did you want anything?"

"What kind of pie do you have?" I asked her.

Trish smiled. "Cherry and apple crumb."

"Is that one kind of pie or two?" I asked her, happy that we were still on good terms.

She laughed at my question. "It's two, but I'll tell you what I'll do. I'll serve you a half slice of each. How does that sound?"

"Great, if you'll make it two," Grace interjected. "After all, I'd hate for those two orphaned half slices to just go to waste."

"Was that 'waste' or 'waist'?" Trish asked her.

"Probably both, but I'll take my chances," Grace answered with a smile.

"Mind if I grab something and join you two?" she asked. I'd promised her lunch with us the next day, but why not do it now?

"That would be great. We can take a few minutes and catch up with each other's lives while Grace is eating," I said.

"I'll be there shortly," Trish said. "Why don't you take this table so I'll be close to the kitchen and the cash register?" she asked as she tapped an empty table near the front.

"That sounds good," I said.

After Grace and I were seated and served a pair of iced teas, though I hadn't requested one, Trish added a glass for herself.

"Did you even want a tea?" Grace asked me softly after the diner owner disappeared into the kitchen.

"You know me. I'm *always* up for tea," I said as I took a sip. I'd probably be bouncing off the walls later from the overload of sugar and caffeine, but I really didn't care. There were some sacrifices worth making.

Trish came out with a large tray a few minutes later, and soon Grace was eating her main meal while Trish and I had our desserts. Trish had chosen banana pudding, and it looked wonderful, but I didn't regret my choice of getting a variety of pie slices. When given the option for dessert, it was a rare day that I ever chose *anything* but pie if it was available.

We chatted about a dozen things as Grace ate, but the moment she started in on her own small pie slices, I asked the grill owner, "Trish, what were you going to say earlier?"

"Earlier than what?" she asked. "Whoops, I have to go. I'll be right back." She left us to ring up a customer as Grace took her first bite of the cherry crumb pie and then followed it up quickly with a bite of the apple crumb.

"Where do you put it?" I asked her in awe. "You're as skinny as a rail no matter what you eat."

"I owe it all to clean living and a positive mental attitude," she answered with a grin. "That and a metabolism like a hummingbird that I inherited from my mother. She could eat anything she pleased and never gain an ounce. I can't quite claim that myself, but I'm not that far off."

"You know what? I'm trying really hard not to hate you right now," I said with a grin, "but it's kind of tough at the moment."

"How could you? After all, I'm the most loveable person I know," she said, and we both started laughing as Trish rejoined us.

"What did I miss?"

"Grace was just telling me how loveable she is," I said with a smile.

"Okay," Trish answered, clearly not getting the joke.

"You were about to say earlier?" I asked her.

"Oh, right. I saw something at ReNEWed yesterday, but I'm not sure that it means anything."

"Why don't you tell us and let us decide?" I asked her.

"Tyra Hitchings was acting odd, and for her, that's saying something. She stormed out of ReNEWed about an hour before I heard the first siren."

"Why would she do that?" I asked. Tyra had once been a wealthy woman who had fallen on hard times recently, and I knew from some comments Gabby had made that Tyra was selling off her nice things a few articles at a time to cover her bills.

"I have a feeling I know. That woman's always had a temper, so it didn't surprise me that she'd be upset with Gabby. Tyra's been selling things to ReNEWed for a while now," Trish said, independently confirming what Gabby had told me. "She usually does it in the store's off hours so no one will see her leaving the place. The only reason I know anything about it at all is that I've spotted her visiting a few times in the past. She goes in with a large bag that's clearly full of clothes, and then she leaves later with nothing but a grim expression on her face. This was the first time I'd ever seen her visit the place during regular business hours."

"I wonder what their argument was about?" Grace asked.

"I've got a feeling I know," I said grimly.

"Why would she be mad?" Trish asked me. "Gabby always pays for what she buys."

"True, but I'm sure it doesn't feel as though it's enough, especially when you see what she turns around and charges for the same things she just bought," I answered. "If that was Tyra's first time in the store itself, she must have been furious to learn how much profit Gabby was making off her things."

"That's pure speculation, and you know it," Grace said as she pushed her dessert plate away.

"Yes, but there's one way to find out. Let's go pay Tyra a call, shall we?"

Trish frowned. "I wish I could go with you, but I've got to stay here and man the register."

"We'll let you know what we find out," I promised.

"You'd better."

As Trish stood and cleared the table, Grace slid a twenty-dollar bill toward her. "That was delightful."

"Twenty is too much," Trish said. "I'll go grab your change."

"Just apply it to my next bill," Grace said with a smile.

"No, ma'am. I'll forget, and then I'll remember, and then I'll be upset," Trish explained.

"Okay, I'll be right here," Grace said. It was pretty clear that she hadn't understood Trish's reasoning, but then again, she'd never owned her own business. She may have had her own set of headaches, but that didn't mean that our lives were worry free. I hated the thought of cheat-

ing someone—whether accidentally or not—more than just about anything, and I knew that Trish felt the same way, too.

After Grace got her change, Trish said with a smile, "If you leave me
a tip, I'll dump a pitcher of tea in your lap."

Grace, who had clearly been considering doing what Trish had just
surmised, quickly tucked the money back into her purse. "I wouldn't
dream of it."

We all laughed about it, and as Grace and I stepped outside, I said,
"Let's take a shortcut through the park and grab my Jeep first. Tyra lives
too far away for us to walk."

"Especially after that meal," Grace said. "I'm not entirely sure I can
make it to your place after everything I just ate."

"You can wait right here, and I can come by and pick you up," I offered with a smile.

"No, if you can make the trek, then so can I," I said.

We headed through the park toward the cottage I shared with Jake,
but something stopped us before we got there.

Someone was standing still, staring oddly at the back of my home,
and I had a creepy feeling that I knew exactly who it was, though why
they were there, I couldn't even begin to guess.

Chapter 8

"Buster Breckenridge, what are you doing here, and why are you staring at my cottage?" I asked the man as he turned around. "I thought you were still in prison."

"Hello, Suzanne," Buster said with a smile that managed to give me chills. He'd been forty pounds heavier the last time I'd seen him, and in the interim, he'd dropped the fat and had gained quite a bit of muscle mass, from the look of him. There was a scar just below his right eye, and his hair was shorter than I'd ever seen it in my life, but there was no mistaking him. "Is that any way to greet an old friend?"

"No, but we've *never* been friends, so it doesn't matter," I said. "I can't believe you have the nerve to show your face in town again after what you did."

He held up his hands and smiled again, but there was no warmth in it at all. "Even though I was innocent, I did my time, Suzanne, and now I'm free to go wherever I please."

"And you chose to come back to April Springs?" I asked him incredulously. "Of all the places in the world, you decided that you wanted to be here?"

"What can I say?" he asked. "I got homesick." He seemed to notice Grace for the first time. "Hey, Gorgeous," he said with a grin. "How's it going? You're looking prettier than ever."

"Don't call me Gorgeous," Grace said as her complexion went ashen at the moment he turned his attention to her. "Does Stephen Grant know you're back?"

"I have no idea. I just got here twenty minutes ago," he said. "Why do you care what Stephen Grant does and does not know?"

"Stephen happens to be the chief of police now, and he's my boyfriend, too," she replied.

"Really? How interesting," Buster said.

"What are you doing standing in the park looking at my house?" I asked him. "If my husband sees you creeping around the place, he's going to make it rough on you."

"Are you talking about Max? Believe me, I'm not worried about that ham of an actor, not after what I've been through," Buster said.

"Max and I are divorced. I'm married to a former State Police Inspector these days," I told him smartly.

"Wow, things really *have* changed since I left town," he said. After a moment, he snapped his fingers and smiled. "I just got it. Donut Hearts. Is that your place?"

"It is," I told him.

Paige must have seen us in the park from the bookstore, because she soon joined us. "Suzanne, I wanted to talk to you about... Hello," she said to Buster, interrupting herself.

"Hi there," Buster said, trying to turn on his charm but failing miserably at it, at least as far as I was concerned. "My name is Buster. And you are?" he asked as he put out a hand.

Paige was about to answer and take it when Grace stepped in between them. "Don't talk to him. He's bad news," she said.

Paige pulled her hand back, looking extremely confused. "I don't understand."

"Buster here burned down a church on the edge of town ten years ago," I explained. "As a matter of fact, it was just like what happened to Gabby's shop yesterday."

"Well, don't look at me. Like I said before, I just got here," Buster said. "Besides, I didn't set either one of those fires. I'm innocent. I was then, and I still am, no matter *what* some people testified to at my trial."

"It seems like an awfully big coincidence though, doesn't it?" Grace asked. "You show up here, and suddenly the whole town catches on fire again?"

"I'd hardly call that old shop the entire town," Buster said. "If it was still like what I remember, *everything* in that building was flammable, but I didn't have anything to do with it."

"You and Gabby never got along though, did you?" I asked him. "When she testified at your trial that she saw you smoking in back of the church, it was enough to get you convicted, and you swore you'd get revenge, didn't you?"

"What can I say? I was young and stupid back then, and I was focusing on the wrong enemy," Buster said. "I shouldn't have to remind you that she wasn't the *only* one who pointed a finger at me in court. I was lashing out at everyone back then. I threatened George Morris for arresting me; do you remember that? How is old George? I imagine he's long dead and in the ground by now."

"Hardly. He's alive and kicking, and as a matter of fact, he's our mayor," I explained.

"This just keeps getting better and better. Well, as much as I'd love to hang around and chat, I've got to get back to Union Square. I've got a job there, and my boss gets a little grumpy if I'm late. See you all around," he said, and then added, "Nice meeting you, ma'am, whatever your name might be."

Buster then walked back to the street, got on a motorcycle, and then sped off.

"What was that all about?" Paige asked. "Did he really burn a church down?"

"Buster denied it at the time, but there was enough proof to convict him. He swore that he'd been set up and that when he got out he'd find out who really did it and make them pay, but nobody believed him."

"How were you involved, Suzanne?" Paige asked me.

"Can I just say that it's a long story and leave it at that?" I asked her.

"I suppose that's your right," Paige said as she started to walk away.

"Hey, you were coming over to talk to us about something," I reminded her. "What's up?"

"It can wait," Paige said. "I'd better get back to the shop."

"Hang on," I said. She was going to find out sooner or later, so I might as well be the one to tell her. "Buster and I have a bit of a history, that's all."

"You two *dated*?" she asked me.

"Hey, *I* went out with him before I knew that he was an arsonist, not Suzanne," Grace protested.

"Sorry, he just didn't seem to have that kind of vibe with her."

"It's fine," I said. "No, I never dated him. The truth is that I testified against him too. Between what Gabby said and my statement in court, he went away for ten years for arson."

"Did you see him smoking at the church, too?" Paige asked as she rejoined us.

"No, but the day before the fire I saw him flicking matches at a trash can by the town clock. When it caught on fire, he laughed about it. I managed to put it out with my water bottle, but it wasn't something I was likely to forget. After he was arrested, I realized that there might be a pattern of him playing with matches, so I came forward. I didn't have much choice. It felt as though it was my civic duty."

"I'm not sure that's how *he* saw it," Grace said. "Remember, he threatened to get you, too."

"There's a whole host of folks in town he has a grudge against," I said, trying to ease the tension that was suddenly in the air. Buster coming back to town was definitely going to make things harder for a great many people. Had he set fire to Gabby's shop, hoping to take my donut shop out with it? He'd pretended to be surprised that I owned Donut Hearts, but what if he knew it all along, and he was trying to settle two scores with one fire?

I needed to tell Jake what was going on, but first I wanted to see what Paige had to say. Maybe she'd seen something at Gabby's the day before that would help us figure out what had really happened to her shop.

Things had suddenly gotten a great deal more complicated with Buster's reappearance, but I wasn't going to let that hamper my investigation. If he *had* been the one to burn ReNEWed down, he'd pay for it. I'd see to that, but if it was someone else, I'd make sure they were the ones who were brought to justice.

Either way, someone was going to pay.

"I really do have to get back to work," Paige said as she started off toward her bookstore.

"We'll come with you," I said as Grace and I tagged along.

"Is there any way that you have a second to talk to us?" I asked Paige as Grace and I walked into the bookstore right behind her. I loved the space, and it was all I could do not to pull a book from the shelves at random and start reading, but Grace and I were on a mission, and any reading I did was going to have to wait.

Paige grabbed a clipboard holding half a dozen computer-printed sheets and started leafing through it. "I'm sorry. I've really got to get this finished."

"Paige, it won't take a second," I said firmly.

She looked at me for a moment, and then she shrugged. "Okay, but I honestly don't have much time."

"We'll take as little as we can," Grace said. "What were you about to tell us outside earlier when you realized that we were speaking with someone else?"

"It's about what happened at ReNEWed," she said. "I heard Mindy Fulbright arguing with Gabby about something yesterday in front of the bank. It's not all that odd for Gabby to have a public disagreement with someone, but given what happened later, I thought it might be important." She lowered her clipboard for a moment. "You two *are* looking into the fire, aren't you?"

"Haven't you heard? The SBI said it was an accident, and Chief Grant isn't arguing the point," I said.

The bookstore owner looked at us both askance. "Come on. I don't believe that any more than you do. How did the fire supposedly start?"

"There was a faulty old toaster oven in back," Grace volunteered.

"Now I *know* it's not true," Paige said. "Gabby wouldn't make anything in that shop, not even a piece of toast."

"That's what we said," I told her, "but nobody seems to care what we think."

"Well, I do," Paige said.

"I didn't realize that you and Gabby were that close," Grace said.

The bookstore owner lowered her voice. "We aren't, but if someone's burning businesses down in April Springs, it matters to me." She paused before adding, "Besides, nobody deserves dealing with that kind of total destruction. Have you heard anything, Suzanne, I mean about Gabby?"

"She's still in critical condition," I said. I wasn't about to share what Penny had told me. Not only did Paige not need to know, but I was still trying to mend my fractured relationship with the nurse.

"That's too bad," Paige said. "Listen, keep me posted, okay? I hate to say this, but I've really got to get back to work."

"No worries," I said. "We'll get out of your hair. There's just one last thing. Did you happen to overhear exactly what Gabby and Mindy were fighting about?"

"Money, from the sound of it," Paige said.

"How so?" I asked.

"I don't have a clue. I guess the only way to find out is to ask Mindy."

"We'll put her on our list," Grace said.

"Thanks for chatting," I added as Grace and I started to leave the bookstore.

"Anytime, except maybe right now," she said with a frown. "I'm truly sorry I can't give you any more time."

"Hey, running your business well is important," I told her.

"So is keeping up with friendships," she answered.

"No worries on that account," I said.

After Grace and I were back outside, she asked, "So, which one do we talk to first?"

"I'd say we start with Tyra and then speak with Mindy," I said. "Do you mind if I call Jake while we're walking to my place to pick up my Jeep?"

"That depends. Do you mind me eavesdropping?" Grace asked me with a grin.

"Have I ever in the past?" I asked with a smile in return.

"Not that I can recall," she said.

I got Jake on the fourth ring. "Is this a bad time?"

"I've got a second," he replied, sounding distinctly out of breath.

"I can check back in with you later," I answered.

"No, I need a breather, and so does my supervisor," he said.

"I said I was sorry," I heard the mayor say in the background.

"I heard you," Jake said, and I could hear footsteps followed by a door opening and slamming shut behind him. "I'm on the porch, and by the way, I wasn't the one who slammed that door. It's got a habit of catching the wind and shutting itself."

"How are you two doing?" I asked him.

"We're fine. We just had a difference of opinion. I wanted to do something the right way, and Mayor Morris wanted to do it his way."

I did my best not to laugh. They were two bullheaded men, and the only thing that amazed me was that they weren't clashing more often than they were. "Do you need a referee?"

"No, we'll be fine. What's up?"

"Listen, do you remember me telling you about Buster Breckenridge a long time ago?"

"The arsonist? Yeah, I remember," Jake replied. "What about him?"

"He's out of prison, and worse yet, he's decided to come back to April Springs," I said. There were a few moments of silence until I started to get uncomfortable. "Jake, are you still here?"

"I am," he said. "Have you seen him yourself?"

"He was in the park, looking at our cottage," I admitted.

"Is he still there?" Jake asked, and I could hear him starting to head back inside.

"Relax. He's on his way to Union Square, where evidently he's working, at what I do not know."

I could hear his footsteps stop. "How did he seem to you?"

"As a matter of fact, he was oddly calm," I told him.

"He might be now, but I read those transcripts right after you told me about him before we were married. He threatened you in open court, Suzanne."

Knowing Jake, I wasn't surprised that he'd researched the case after I'd told him about it. "Jake, he threatened a great many people, including the mayor, but he claims that he's a changed man."

"I know some folks can change, but it's a lot harder than most people think," Jake said. "I need to tell the mayor. Could you hold on for one second?"

"Sure," I said. He muffled the receiver so I couldn't hear what he was saying, so I turned to Grace. "He's telling George."

"That's a good idea," Grace said. "I'd hate for something to happen to the mayor."

"Do you believe that Buster started the fire at ReNEWed?" I asked her.

"No," she said. "I don't."

I was about to ask her why when Jake came back onto the line. "Okay, he knows."

"What did he say?"

"He told me that if Buster wants trouble, he'll get more than he can handle," Jake said. "Suzanne, I don't like this."

"Jake, there's nothing we can do about it. I'm not worried."

"Well, maybe you should be," he said.

I thought about it, and then I asked him, "In your expert opinion, if he started the fire at Gabby's yesterday, would he really allow himself to be seen around town today?"

He gave it some thought before answering. "It all depends on what kind of guy he is," Jake finally said. "What do you think?"

"I don't know," I answered honestly.

"I don't either, but I'm going to talk to him and find out." I didn't like that tone of voice, the deadness to his words that always scared me.

"Jake, he was right when he said that he served his time. Remember, you're not a cop anymore."

"Believe me, I'm well aware of that fact. There's nothing that says we can't have a nice polite conversation though, is there?"

"I don't suppose so," I said. "Listen, I want to talk to you about something else." I wanted to ask him about Chief Grant's suggestion that Jake help the Union Square police chief out with his robbery investigations.

"Can it wait until tonight? The mayor is inside slamming things around again."

"It can wait. Be careful, okay?"

He chuckled softly. "Right back at you."

Our talk would have to wait until later after all.

"What were you about to say?" I asked Grace as I put my cell phone away.

"It doesn't matter anymore," she said.

"Of course it does. Go on. I'm listening."

"I was going to suggest the same thing you just did to your husband. Why on earth would Buster stick around after torching ReNEWed? It just doesn't sound as though it's something an arsonist would do, at least as far as I'm concerned."

"I'm not saying that we should take his name off the list entirely, but it does seem a bit odd, doesn't it?"

"It's something to consider, anyway," she said as we approached my Jeep. "Do you need to go inside for anything before we get into this?"

"No, I'm ready to roll if you are."

"Then let's go see what Tyra Hitchings and Mindy Fulbright have to say for themselves."

Chapter 9

"**H**i, Tyra. Do you have a second?" I asked the older woman—elegantly dressed but looking a bit haggard—as she answered her front door. The house had once been stately, neatly painted and carefully landscaped, but it was clear from the outside that it, like its owner, had fallen on hard times. Tyra herself was still dressed nicely, but I was willing to bet that the clothes she was wearing hadn't been bought new for several seasons.

"Sorry, but I'm in a bit of a rush," she said as she tried to block our view of the foyer.

"I understand," I said as I leaned in and peered inside, trying to get a better look. "Woops. Sorry about that," I said as I forced the door open. "Are you going somewhere?" There were four large pieces of luggage stacked near the door.

"Those bags? No, I'm clearing out my closets and my attic and donating some things to charity," she said as she bit her lower lip.

"The prospect of making ends meet now that Gabby's shop is gone must be tough for you," Grace said.

Tyra frowned at her, and I could see her temper start to flare before she pulled herself back in. "Grace, I'm sure I don't know what you're talking about."

"Come on, it's common knowledge that you've been selling your things to ReNEWed for months now," Grace said. "There's no shame in it, Tyra. I've done it myself a time or two."

"As I said, I'm making a rather large donation of things I don't need anymore. I'm planning on downsizing, and in order to do that, a great deal of my things have to go first. I've been rattling around in this big old house by myself for much too long. Sometimes I feel as though I'm serving it and not the other way around. What do I need with five bedrooms and three bathrooms? I live alone, for goodness' sake. Streamlining my life is the *only* reason I've dropped a few things off at Gabby's recently. I've got to do *something* with all of this stuff," she said. "Now if you'll excuse me, I really must attend to some things."

"We're sorry to bother you," I said as the door started to close. "We thought we'd give you the courtesy of checking with you first, but if you're so busy, we'll just go by and talk to the police chief and tell him."

The door never made it all the way closed as Tyra opened it again quickly. "What are you talking about?" There was definitely a hint of temper in her voice, and while so far she'd managed to control it pretty well, it was still clearly there. Then again, I might have gotten annoyed myself if someone were pressing me like we were pushing her.

"Someone spotted you arguing with Gabby yesterday before the fire in front of her shop," I said.

"And we just happen to have it from other sources that you've been sneaking around selling things for quite some time," Grace added. Okay, our source for both pieces of information was Trish Granger, but we weren't about to give our friend's name to this woman.

"I'm sorry, but that is complete and utter nonsense," she said crossly. "Certainly I had words with Gabby. The woman is as abrasive as steel wool. I challenge you to find five people in all of April Springs who haven't had some sort of altercation with Gabby Williams in the past."

She had a point, but I couldn't let logic interfere with our questioning. "Then you should be fine. Gabby keeps a complete set of records of everyone she bought from. You knew that, didn't you?" I asked. It was true as far as it went. I knew Gabby liked to keep lists, but whether she'd ever compiled the names into one place I didn't know, at least not for sure.

"If she did, wouldn't they have been burned up in the fire as well?" Tyra asked.

"A year ago maybe, but Gabby's getting to be pretty computer savvy these days. It wouldn't surprise me a bit to find out that the information is out there in cyberspace just waiting for the police. You might as well admit it up front to us. Maybe we can help you," I said. Gabby's extent of computer awareness was filling out some dating site profiles, at least as far as I knew. I was way out on a limb at the moment, and it would just take a second for Tyra to call me on it.

But she didn't.

"Fine," the woman admitted wearily. "As you said yourself, there's nothing to be ashamed of. I've sold an odd item here and there to her over the past several months. At first I wanted to test the waters, but lately I've been selling more and more to her. And why shouldn't I? Let someone else enjoy the things I don't need or want anymore." She gestured to the bags. "The money it's brought has been a nice bonus, and while I feel good when I donate to charity, as I said, this house doesn't pay for itself. I have money, ladies, but who wouldn't like a little more to help make ends meet? So what if we did business together?" She looked at Grace. "You said yourself that you've done the same thing."

"Maybe, but I didn't storm out of ReNEWed hours before it burned to the ground," Grace said serenely. "What were you so upset about?"

Tyra sighed heavily. Clearly we were trying her patience. Well, it wouldn't be the first time someone was tired of our questioning, and I was sure it wouldn't be the last, either. She was still standing in the doorway blocking us, and now she sighed and crumpled a little. "I decided to see just how much she was getting for my things. It was a matter of curiosity more than anything else. Did you know she marks up everything she takes in at an outrageous amount? She made three times more than she ever paid me. I didn't feel that it was fair, and I told her so."

"What did she say in response to that?" I asked her. It was as I'd expected earlier, but it was nice getting confirmation from her about my theory.

"Gabby told me in no uncertain terms that I was invited to see if I could do better on my own if I didn't like her terms. We both knew that wasn't going to happen, so I dropped it and left. By the time I got back here, I started to see her point. After all, I hadn't been under any obligation to accept her offers. I decided that getting something for my things was much better than just donating them, as good as that might have made me feel. Ultimately I came to the conclusion that I'd overreacted, so I was going to go back over there and apologize, but I never got the chance," she added wistfully.

"Was that the last time you saw Gabby," Grace asked her, "or did you happen to see her later?"

After a split second, Tyra said, "No, unfortunately that was the last time I saw her alive."

"Tyra, Gabby's not dead yet, unless you know something that we don't," I told her.

The older woman looked genuinely shocked by the revelation. "What? Tilly Ranger from next door came over last night to help me pack up those bags, and she told me that ReNEWed was gone, burned to the ground. She said that Gabby had been inside at the time, so I just assumed that she was dead. What great news! I'm relieved she made it out in time. How is the poor thing? I hated the thought that the last thing I said to her was said in anger. She might not have been my favorite person in the world, but I still didn't want that argument on my conscience."

"I wouldn't be surprised if she makes a complete recovery," I lied. I was trying to get a reaction out of Tyra.

"Then I've got a chance to make things right with her after all? That's excellent. Do you happen to know if she's home right now? I've got to apologize and clear my conscience as soon as possible."

"Actually, they're keeping her at the hospital for observation," I said, which on the face of it was actually true. I was sure while she was in intensive care, they were observing her most carefully.

"Do you happen to know if they will let her have visitors?"

"I'm not sure," I said.

"After the truck comes to pick up those bags, I'll pick up some flowers and see if I can get a minute of her time." She smiled. "I've got to say, I'm quite relieved to find out I was wrong. That Tilly. I should have known that she'd exaggerate the situation! I appreciate you stopping by, ladies."

I was about to ask her a follow-up question when a large truck from Goodwill pulled into the driveway. I could still get out, but just barely.

"That's the truck I was waiting for. Thanks again," she said as two husky men got out of the truck and approached us.

"Where are the things you wanted to donate, Mrs. Hitchings?" one of the men said.

"They're by the door, but I have some furniture in the house, too."

It was clear that Tyra was indeed making a donation and not going anywhere. My overactive imagination had jumped to a conclusion when I'd seen those bags, and I'd been proved wrong. It was entirely possible that everything Tyra had told us was true. I'd had more than my share of public rows with Gabby myself. If that fire had occurred right after one of our arguments, I would be the one under intense scrutiny, not Tyra. "Come on, Grace. Let's go."

"What do you think?" I asked Grace after I managed to get the Jeep out of the driveway without hitting anything. "Was she telling us the truth?"

"Her explanations all made sense," Grace allowed, "but there are facts that still cast her in a bad light. That fight alone is reason to keep her on our list of suspects."

"We've both had arguments with Gabby in public in the past, but that doesn't mean that we were the ones who torched the place," I reminded her.

"Trust me, I know that more than anyone else in town, probably," she allowed. "Still, the timing of it all looks bad."

"I think she genuinely felt bad about the fight, given what happened afterwards," I persisted. "You've got to admit that she wanted to find Gabby and apologize as soon as she found out she was still alive."

Grace nodded. "You were playing kind of fast and loose with the truth there, weren't you? Don't get me wrong. I'm not scolding you, Suzanne. I thought it was a nice touch."

"I wanted to see how she reacted," I admitted.

"I just wish that I had thought to do it myself," Grace admitted with a smile. "But then again, that's why there are two of us."

As she took out her cell phone, I asked, "Who are you calling?"

"I want to tell Stephen what's going on," she admitted.

"I've already told him that we were investigating," I reminded her.

"I told him, too, but I promised to keep him updated, and I just realized that I hadn't told him what Trish shared with us. You don't mind, do you?"

"I'm not sure there's enough to report just yet, but I'm fine if you want to tell him," I said as I started driving toward Mindy Fulbright's place.

"When it comes to keeping my relationship with him on solid ground, I'd rather err on the side of caution," she said. "After all, he's the police chief, and he has a right to know what's going on."

"Grace, I don't have much time to talk. What's up?" the chief asked as he answered her call. She'd put it on speaker so we could both talk to him, which I appreciated. Sometimes it was very frustrating having to listen in on half a conversation and try to fill in the blanks about what the other person was saying.

"Suzanne and I are just leaving Tyra Hitchings's place," she told him.

"Okay. *Why* exactly should that matter to me?"

"It's Suzanne, Chief. We found out that Tyra had an argument with Gabby yesterday before the fire," I told Chief Grant. "From what an eyewitness told us, she was extremely upset about it."

"Which one was upset, Gabby or Tyra?" the chief asked.

"Tyra," I amended. "We never actually got a report on Gabby's state of mind. Anyway, it might not be a bad idea to talk to her when you get a chance."

"About?" he asked, the question hanging in the air like a low cloud. It was pretty clear that his patience was wearing thin.

"The fire, and the attack on Gabby," Grace said bluntly.

"Ladies, need I remind you that the fire, and Gabby's condition, were both due to an accident, not arson?" the chief asked.

"So you say," Grace said, "but what would it hurt to drop by her place and have a friendly chat with her about it?"

"Listen, is there any way that we can talk about this later? Something's come up. Suzanne, you should probably hear this, too, since it concerns you as well."

"Is it about Buster Breckinridge?" I asked him. "Because if it is, we already know that he's back in town. As a matter of fact, we talked to him in the park an hour ago."

"Did he say anything to you, Grace?" the chief asked her tensely.

"He called me 'Gorgeous,'" Grace admitted.

"Well, that much is certainly true enough. Suzanne, you need to be careful. You remember his threats, right?"

"I'm not likely to forget them," I admitted. "I already told Jake about what happened."

"What did he have to say?"

"He told me that he was going to find Buster at his earliest convenience, and that the two men were going to have a little chat," I said.

"I'll just bet they are," the chief said, a hint of delight in his voice. "I wouldn't mind being invited to that particular conversation myself."

"Jake promised me that he'd keep things civil," I said, suddenly worried about my husband's state of mind when it came to my welfare. Jake had a habit of being a bit overprotective of me, and while I normally didn't mind it, at the moment, it might make things a little more difficult for all of us.

"I'll just bet he did," the chief said. "Listen, if there's nothing else I can do for you, I've got to get back to work. Thanks for checking in with me."

"You bet," Grace said. "Will I see you tonight?"

"I'll call you later," he answered as he signed off.

After she put her phone away, Grace asked me, "I wonder what story we'll get out of Mindy?"

"I don't know, but I'm dying to find out. Let's go see what she has to say for herself about her argument with Gabby. I have a hunch the more we dig into this, the more folks we're going to find who had a bone to pick with her."

Chapter 10

"Mindy, we'd like to talk to you about Gabby Williams," I said as Mindy Fulbright answered her door. She was a little older than Gabby, somewhere in her early sixties, and her fashion sense was more like my casual attire than Gabby's. Still, she was quite lovely, tall and thin, almost regal in her bearing. Her home was certainly in better shape than Tyra's had been, though not nearly so grand. It seemed just about the right size for one or two people, whereas Tyra must have really rattled around in her fading palace. Seeing Mindy's place, I could certainly understand Tyra's desire to downsize.

"Did she die?" Mindy asked hesitantly.

"Not as far as we know," Grace said. "Would it really bother you that much if she had?"

I thought that was way too harsh right out of the gate. "What Grace means is that we heard you two had an argument about money a few days ago."

Mindy looked genuinely perplexed by my statement. "I don't have any earthly idea what you are talking about, Suzanne. Why on earth would Gabby and I argue about money?"

"That's just what we heard," I backpedaled quickly. Was it possible that Paige had gotten it wrong? I knew my bookselling friend, and she wasn't one to say things without reason. "Then you're saying that it's *not* true that you were fighting over money?"

"Money? No. Oh, I see. I suppose that makes sense," she replied.

"Maybe to you, but we're more in the dark than ever," Grace said truthfully. "If you weren't fighting over money, what were you arguing about?"

"You might as well come in," Mindy said. "It's a long and sordid story, and I don't care to tell it out on my front porch."

"Thanks," I said as we walked inside after her. I knew that most times, actually being invited in was a major achievement in the course of our investigations, so at least Mindy was cooperating that much.

"Would you ladies like some tea?" she offered. "I was just about to have some."

"We're good," I said quickly. "This won't take long."

"Unfortunately, time is something I've got too much of these days," Mindy said. "Ever since Henry died, I seem to be at a loss as to how to fill my life with meaning. I tried going back to work, but I just couldn't bear it. Besides, Henry was a thoughtful man, always trying to plan for the worst-case scenario in case something ever happened to one of us. He never planned on getting run over by a teenaged girl asleep at the wheel while he was out on his morning stroll, but he left me more than comfortable, at least as far as money was concerned."

"So, if you weren't arguing about money, what was it?" Grace asked.

"Manny," she said with a frown.

"Manny? Who is he?" I asked.

"It's a long story. At first I thought he was sent to me from heaven, but the more I've found out about him lately, the more likely I believe his origins began in the opposite direction." She looked down at her hands, which were clutching an old linen handkerchief. "This is embarrassing to admit, but I've been lonely since Henry died, so I decided to do something about it."

"There's no need to be embarrassed about that," I said quickly. "We understand how lonely life can be sometimes."

"Do you really, though? Suzanne, I know you've been through a divorce, and as painful as that must have been, Henry left me unwillingly. There's been a void in my life ever since, and one of my friends from my bridge group told me about an online dating site for folks my age. It's difficult meeting new people, so I thought I'd give it a try. Manny seemed sweet, and he was very handsome, so I agreed to go out with him. However, we'd been dating for over a month when I found out that Manny was seeing quite a few other women as well."

"Pardon me for saying so, but that's not all that unusual, is it? After all, you hadn't known each other that long," I said.

"That's true enough, but when I began to dig a little deeper into his life, I learned that he was engaged to at least three women he'd met on the same dating service I'd been using, and evidently he had other women lined up as well."

"Including Gabby," Grace and I said at nearly the same time. I liked to think that I'd been a half step ahead of her, but I couldn't swear to it.

"Yes, including Gabby. In fact, she was the first 'other woman' I discovered. I wanted to confront Manny, but I couldn't find him anywhere, so naturally I went to speak with Gabby. Let me tell you, she was not pleased with me when I attacked her. I'm afraid I told her that Manny was mine and that she needed to find someone else. Gabby responded by threatening me, and I returned her harsh words in kind. It was a very ugly scene, and I felt bad about how I'd reacted almost immediately. You see, Manny had told me that *I* was the only woman he'd ever been able to love since his wife died. It turns out that he'd been divorced four times, but never *widowed*. I know I must sound like a perfect fool, but when I was with him, I found myself overwhelmed by the level of his intensity. It was as though I was the only other person in the world when we were together, and I'm afraid I fell for it completely and utterly."

I reached out and patted her hand. "You can't blame yourself for trusting someone to be who they claimed to be," I said.

"At my age, I should have known better," she said. "Anyway, I went to see Gabby to confront her, and evidently she'd thought she'd been exclusive with Manny as well. We had an argument that got fairly intense, and those were the last words I ever spoke to her. I've been wracked with guilt ever since I heard about the fire and her condition."

"What about Manny? Did you ever get in touch with him?"

Mindy's expression turned icy. "After fighting with Gabby, I no longer cared to speak with him ever again. I texted him and told him that we were through. I couldn't even trust myself to tell him face to face. It was cowardly of me, I know, but the man is so charming that I wasn't completely certain that I could resist him, even after everything I'd found out."

"Did he answer you?" I asked her.

She pulled out her cell phone and showed the text to us. All it said was 'Your loss.' Evidently he wasn't all that charming.

"I do hope Gabby recovers."

"So do we," I said.

"Mindy, was that argument the last time you saw Gabby?" Grace asked.

"Yes, I'm afraid it was."

"Okay then," Grace said as she stood up. I did as well, but before we left, I asked her, "Do you happen to know where we can find Manny?"

"Of course. He lives in Union Square. Do you know where the Moorcroft Garden Center is on the edge of town?"

"I do," I said. I'd bought a few plants there once, but they'd quickly died upon transplanting, so I'd never gone back.

"He owns the place, so that's probably where you'll find him, if he's not out already looking for replacements for both Gabby and me."

Once we were out in the Jeep, Grace looked at me and asked, "You bought her story hook, line, and sinker, didn't you?"

"What are you talking about?" I asked her. "Do you *not* believe that Mindy was wronged by that man?"

"Suzanne, I couldn't love you any more if you were my flesh-and-blood sister, but you have a fatal flaw."

"What might that be?" I asked. "Please, enlighten me."

"You tend to want to believe the best in people," she said simply, as though she were stating a universal truth and not just her opinion.

"And you don't?"

"Sometimes," Grace admitted, "but do me a favor and think about it. Mindy had to know that she'd been caught fighting with Gabby in public before ReNEWed burned down. She also had to realize that if something happened to Gabby, *someone* would dig into her love life as a matter of course, which would have produced Manny, and a connection would be made between the two women."

"I don't know. That sounds like a bit of a stretch to me," I said as we got into the Jeep and headed for Union Square.

"Not really, not if anyone worth their salt was investigating the case," Grace said. "From the way Mindy was spinning the story, it would be impossible to believe that she had anything to do with the fire."

I didn't want to admit to Grace that based on the interview we'd just had with Mindy, I'd already struck her name from our list of suspects in my mind. Grace was right. I did have a tendency to want to believe the best in people, and Mindy's story had been quite skillfully told. "Okay, I can see your point. How do you think that it might have happened?"

"I'm not saying that it occurred this way, but isn't it just as likely that Mindy and Gabby fought over Manny's affections, neither one knowing that they weren't by any stretch of the imagination his only conquests? If Mindy was desperate to hold onto Manny, she could burn the shop down to thwart Gabby, whether she realized the owner was inside ReNEWed at the time or not. Then again, she could have continued the fight inside, hit Gabby in the head with whatever blunt object happened to be lying around when she turned her back on her, and then, thinking she'd killed her, burned the place down to cover her tracks?"

"That's a lot of ifs," I said.

"Yes, but it makes more sense to me than *Mindy's* version of what happened," Grace said. "We need to keep digging into her life and see if there have been any other outbursts in her past that might show a tendency toward violence."

I glanced over at her for a second. "Do you honestly believe that woman we just spoke with is capable of doing what you've described?"

"Maybe not the woman we saw, but there's no telling if Mindy's hiding another side from the rest of the world."

"Okay, I know the saying about a woman scorned and all, but *Manny* wasn't attacked, Gabby was."

"That could be only because Manny wasn't available," Grace reminded me. "Besides, you read about it in the papers all of the time. A woman catches her husband cheating with another woman, but instead of going after the man, she attacks the other girl! If I were ever in that situation, I'd team up with her and make sure he never made that mistake again."

"I don't doubt it for a moment," I said. "Manny sounds like a real prize, doesn't he?"

"I can't imagine anyone preying on lonely women in their sixties. Is he doing it for the power trip, or is he after something a bit more financial?"

"It could be a little bit of both," I said, "but we won't know for sure until we ask him."

"Are we going to use aliases as covers when we talk to him?" Grace asked me eagerly. She loved it when we masqueraded as other people.

"No, I think straight on is the best way to go after him," I replied.

Grace was clearly disappointed with my response. "Why is that?"

"For one thing, he'd never believe it if we came in there and started flirting with him," I said with a shrug.

"I don't know. If his ego is as big as it appears to be, he might actually expect us to do just that," Grace said with a grin. "Who knows? We might even be able to use that to our advantage."

"Thanks, but no thanks," I said.

"Why not? Do you have a problem with women our age dating older men?" she asked me. "After all, Jake is older than you are, and you married him."

"By seven years," I said, "not twenty or thirty. Anyway, that's not the point. Manny is a user, plain and simple, going after vulnerable and lonely older women. Age isn't even a factor here. What he does to their *hearts* makes my skin crawl, and that has *nothing* to do with his age."

"Okay, I can see that," Grace said. "So then, how are we going to approach him? Are we going to tackle him head on the moment we see him?"

"I'm not sure we have much choice," I admitted. "If he's a tenth as smooth as Mindy believes he is, we're not going to be able to finesse him into telling us the truth. I think our *only* shot of getting anything useful at all out of him is to catch him off guard."

"Woo-hoo!" Grace said. "Now that I think about it, that sounds like more fun than using fake names."

"I thought you'd like that," I said.

"You know me too well, Suzanne," she answered with a grin.

Chapter 11

"Excuse me, are you Manny Wright?" I asked the older gentleman with silver hair and a ready smile. He was in the process of flirting with a young woman who was barely into her twenties, wearing a sundress and sporting a troubling intrigued look from all of the attention. The garden center not only offered plants of many shapes and sizes but everything anyone would need to start a plot of their own. There were fertilizers, sprays, and dusts everywhere, more chemicals than a lab would ever need. I had to wonder if there were any long-term health risks working around so many dangerous products, but clearly it hadn't dulled the shine of Manny's smile one iota.

"Yes, I'm Mr. Wright," he said as he winked at the young woman, basically ignoring us both as he fixed his gaze on his latest prey.

"Is that what all of your fiancés call you?" Grace asked with a sweet smile, hammering him with it immediately.

"Did you say fiancés?" the young woman asked.

"Evidently there is a whole host of them," I said as I nodded in agreement.

"Sorry. I've got to go," she said as she put the tomato plant that had been in her hands down and hurried away.

Once she had made her escape, the garden center owner turned and finally looked at us. "What do you two want?" he asked, his charm now gone completely. "Did Helen send you?"

"No. Who's Helen?" Grace asked. "Is she another member of your harem?"

"Hardly. We went out on two dates, and now she thinks she owns me," Manny said. "If you're not here on her behalf, why are you here?"

"Do you really have to ask?" I posited. "Did you know that even as we speak, Gabby Williams is in the hospital, fighting for her life?"

He looked surprised to hear the news. "Gabby? What happened to her?"

"Do you honestly care?" Grace asked him. "I'm sure you have more than enough women in your life to keep you busy even without our friend."

It surprised me to hear Grace refer to Gabby as her friend, too. The women had never really gotten along, but then again, when it came to rallying against the cads of the world, I supposed that we were all friends.

"Hey, I care about each and every one of the women I've dated," Manny protested.

"If that were true, why would you propose to so many of them and yet still continue to go trolling for more on the Internet? What are you after, anyway? Are you trying to get money out of them, or is it strictly a power thing? Seriously, answer the question, because I honestly want to know."

"Hey, is it my fault that there aren't enough men my age to go around?" he asked. "For the record, *I* never proposed to any of them. They all asked *me* to marry them."

"And yet you kept saying yes, didn't you? Aren't you willing to take *any* responsibility for your behavior?" Grace asked him.

"I'm sorry, but I don't remember signing up for this lecture. I'll ask you one more time, and then I'm throwing both of you out. Why are you here?"

"Did Gabby get too close to you? Was she too demanding? Is that why you set fire to her shop yesterday, with her in it?" Grace absolutely hammered him with her questions, a staccato of punches that left him reeling.

He took a step backward as though he was trying to ward off a physical blow. "I would never do anything like that! There was a fire?"

"Where were you yesterday between the hours of six and seven p.m.?" I asked him. From what Chief Grant had told me earlier in the day, that was the time the fire had to have started, after Gabby had closed the shop and before someone first spotted the smoke coming out of her building.

"I was here," he said. "Ask anybody."

I pointed to the sign above the door. "It says your hours are seven a.m. to five p.m. That would give you plenty of time to lock the doors, drive to April Springs, and then set the fire."

"I was working in back, repotting some fall flowers," he said as he pointed to a row of seedlings that were barely big enough to plant, at least in my limited experience.

"Was anyone else with you, by any chance?" I asked him.

"Just my helper," he said, and then he turned to a man who had his head buried in a stack of fertilizer. I hadn't even noticed him when we'd come in, but when he turned around, I knew who it was instantly.

Evidently Buster Breckinridge, our local arsonist, was Manny Wright's newest employee.

"Buster, what are you doing here?" I asked him.

"I'm working," he said, not making eye contact with us at all.

"Buster, do you know these women?" Manny asked his employee.

"We've met," he said. "Listen, boss, I need to move those plants we've got out front under cover before it starts pouring. They'll never survive a downpour. Is it okay if I do it now?"

"Fine by me," he said.

Grace smiled at him as she said, "If you won't tell your boss how we know you, we'll be more than glad to do it for you."

That stopped Buster in his tracks. He walked over to us, and I noticed that a few folks in the garden center were more interested in our conversation than they were in what they had been shopping for. Keeping his voice low, he asked, "Is it okay with you two if the whole town doesn't know my history?"

"That all depends on you," I said. "Does Manny know?"

"That he's an ex-con? Yeah, I know. Listen, the man served his time. He deserves a fresh start."

"If he's truly reformed, sure, I agree with that, but ask him about threatening Gabby, our mayor, and even Suzanne here when he was found guilty of arson."

"Is that true?" Manny asked him.

"Yes, but you've got to believe me, I'm a changed man."

"So you say," Manny answered skeptically.

"Don't fire me, boss," Buster said. "I need this job."

Manny seemed to consider the plea, and then he shrugged. "Fine, but stay away from matches when you're at work, do you read me?"

"Yes, sir," he said as he hurried away, but not before giving Grace and me a troubling look. Clearly the felon wasn't happy about us stumbling across him at work, but it had indeed been a coincidence.

"Listen, I give ex-cons a break whenever I can," Manny said.

"That's admirable of you, but is he really your only alibi?" Grace asked him.

"Yes. I can't do anything about that, but it's true."

"And you were together the entire time?" I asked him. "If we check around, is there any chance that we're going to discover that you haven't been completely honest with us? It's better if you tell us now before we make our report to the police." I knew that I was making our investigation sound much more official than it was, since we weren't sanctioned to be doing what we were doing in any way, but I had to use any advantage that I could.

"Well, I ate by myself," Manny reluctantly admitted.

"From when to when?" I asked him.

"I took off at five and got back here around seven," he finally said.

"So you don't have an alibi, and neither does Buster," I said.

"I guess not, but I didn't start any fires. I wasn't in love with Gabby, but she was good company, and I never would have hurt her."

"I hope for your sake that you're telling us the truth," Grace said.

"Listen, I'm done talking to the two of you. If you're not going to buy something, you need to take off."

Grace looked at the plants for a moment, and then stared Manny in the eye. "*Nothing* looks all that good to me here." She turned to me and asked, "How about you, Suzanne?"

"Me, either," I said. As we walked out, I grabbed Grace's arm. "Let's talk to Buster before Manny realizes that we're still here. I want to see if he confirms his boss's story."

"I ate a sandwich in the back, and then I started working," Buster said after we cornered him and asked him for his own alibi.

"You didn't go out?" I asked him.

"On what he pays me? Not hardly. I had a peanut butter and jelly sandwich and a can of soda. Manny didn't get back until just before seven, and then we worked until ten. Listen, if he catches me talking to you, he might decide that I'm more trouble than I'm worth and cut me loose. Do you have any idea how hard it is to get a job as an ex-con? It's a condition of my parole, so I can't afford to lose it."

If he was innocent, which I was in no way certain of quite yet, I didn't want to play a part in sending him back to prison. "Fine. If we need you later, will you still be here?"

"As long as he lets me stay," he said as he finished moving the tender young plants in question. "I've got to get back in there."

After he walked back inside, I looked at Grace. "Evidently I'm too soft, so I need to know if you believe him or not." I said it with a smile, but Grace could tell that she'd stepped a bit over the line with me when she'd told me that earlier.

"Suzanne, you're better at figuring these things out than I'll ever be. I just meant that sometimes your desire to see the best in people is a liability instead of an asset. That's why we make such a good team."

"Okay, I can see that. I'm guessing that you won't be surprised when I tell you that I believe both of them."

"That they ate alone?" Grace asked me carefully.

"No, that there are holes in both of their alibis," I said. "Whatever they were doing from six to seven last night, they weren't doing it together."

"I agree with you a thousand percent," she said. "So they both need to stay on our list."

"They do. Manny is not quite the saint he paints himself to be, is he?"

"As far as I'm concerned, he needs to be squashed like a bug," Grace said in disgust.

"But that doesn't make him an arsonist, or an attempted murderer, either," I reminded her.

"No, but wouldn't it be nice if it worked out that way?" she asked me with a grin.

"It would," I admitted, "but real life is seldom so neatly wrapped up for us, is it?"

"Not so far, but I'm still hoping," she said. "Say, isn't that your husband's truck coming our way?"

I looked up to see Jake driving into the parking lot. He looked as surprised to see us as we were to see him, and I couldn't wait to hear what he was doing in Union Square at the moment.

"Okay, before you start in on me," Jake said the moment he got out and approached us, "let the record show that I am here just to have a nice quiet conversation with Buster about hanging around you and our cottage."

"Jake, maybe you're being a little bit overprotective, don't you think?" I asked him as I kissed him quickly. "Not that I'm complaining that you're looking out for my welfare, but I'm a grown woman. I can take care of myself."

"Trust me, I know that more than just about anybody," he said, "but I didn't think it would hurt to let him know that I'd be around."

I thought about how spooked Buster had been earlier about losing his job. If Jake showed up and started hounding the man, there was little doubt in my mind that Manny would fire him, and if he hadn't been the one to set fire to Gabby's shop, I didn't want him to lose his last chance of being rehabilitated. I supposed in some people's eyes that would make me soft, but I didn't care. I believed in my heart that people had the capacity to change, whether they were willing to put in the hard work to make it happen or not. "Tell you what," I said. "Why don't we put a pin in it for now. If I see him near the house again, you can do your thing, and you won't hear a peep out of me."

"Fine, but if I catch him anywhere near the park or the donut shop, I'm going after him," Jake said.

"Okay," I said. "Hey, while we're all here, why don't we go to Napoli's and get a quick bite for dinner before we head back home?" It had been on my mind ever since we'd entered the city limits of Union Square, and I knew that the restaurant was never far from Grace or Jake's minds, either.

"You two go on," Grace said. "I'll be fine."

"Seriously? You *have* to come with us," I said.

Jake looked at her intently. "Grace, if anyone's a third wheel here, it's me. If it would make you feel better, I'll head back, and you two can go by yourselves."

"You'd do that for me?" Grace asked.

"I didn't say that it would be easy," Jake admitted with a grin, "but your friendship is more important to me than eating at Napoli's. Not a lot, but enough," he added.

"So we'll be three for dinner, I guess," Grace said with a laugh. "There is no way I could live with myself if I made you miss the DeAngelis women, or their cooking."

"Whew, thanks for not calling my bluff," Jake said with a smile. "I'd like to think I have the character to follow up on that promise, but I'm glad you didn't make me test it."

Chapter 12

"Hello, Suzanne. Your ears must have been burning," Angelica DeAngelis said the moment she saw me walk into her restaurant with Jake and Grace.

"Why's that?" I asked her after giving her a hug. I noticed Jake looking envious about the attention I was getting, but why shouldn't he? Angelica was a classic Italian beauty, and even if the food at Napoli's hadn't been outstanding, which it was, I was sure they'd stay busy because of the lovely DeAngelis women running the place, though none of Angelica's daughters could quite match her beauty.

"I had a customer earlier complaining that they couldn't get a good donut anymore," she said. "He was ranting and raving about the standardization of the treat, and I told him if he wanted a real pastry experience, he needed to drive to April Springs and visit you at Donut Hearts."

"Thanks for the referral," I said with a grin. "Are you working the front of the restaurant this evening?"

"For the moment," she said with a sigh. "Sophia has decided that she manages fine without me, so we're giving it a trial run." Lowering her voice, she added, "My daughters conspired to send me on a singles cruise, if you can believe it. It appears they are under the impression that I can't get a date on my own."

"I'd be glad to tell them they're crazy if you'd like me to," Jake said with a smile. "I know a dozen men who would jump at the chance to take you out."

She patted his cheek. "You're sweet, but where are they? I'm not exactly overwhelmed with suitors."

"I don't understand it. In fact, I know for sure that George Morris is interested in you," Jake admitted. "You know our mayor, don't you?"

"Yes, I certainly do," she said, and she actually blushed a bit as she admitted it. "He seems interested enough whenever he comes by, and I like him quite a lot, but he's yet to ask me out."

"He's afraid to," Jake explained. "I'm helping him remodel his lake house, and he was talking about you not the day before yesterday."

She sighed. "And yet here I am, working another night alone."

"You're hardly alone," I said. "How are your daughters?"

"They are wonderful, frustrating, a joy in my life, and an absolute pain in my neck," she said with a smile. "In other words, they are perfect." She grabbed three menus and then led us to a table.

After we were seated, Antonia joined us with sweet teas we hadn't even ordered. "Hey, guys. Do you need a few minutes, or do you know what you'd like?"

We ordered our meals, and as we were sipping our sweet teas, waiting for the food to arrive, I asked Jake, "Is the mayor going to be upset when he finds out that you told Angelica that he has a crush on her?"

"Who's going to tell him? I doubt she'll say anything to him, and I trust the two of you not to. Besides, who cares if he finds out? I think they'd be perfect together, but she's so lovely he's intimidated."

"It's hard to believe that *anything* would intimidate George," I said. "He's never been shy about dating women before. In fact, since he's become mayor, he has no end of women interested in him."

"True, but none of them have been on a level with Angelica," Jake said.

"It sounds like you've got a bit of a crush on her yourself," Grace teased my husband.

He reached across the table and took my hand. "I've already found my love," he said.

"But if you were single?" I asked him with a smile.

He shrugged. "Truthfully, I can't say what I'd do. Angelica is a force of nature, you know?"

"Oh, we know," I said, "but it's sweet of you to hedge your bets. I notice you didn't answer Grace's question." My husband blushed a bit, and I decided not to tease him any more about it. "Jake Bishop, if you didn't have a bit of a crush on Angelica DeAngelis, I'd be worried about you. She's amazing. I might just have to have a little chat with George the next time I see him."

"Are you matchmaking again, Suzanne?" Grace asked me.

"I like to think of it more like me giving a gentle nudge in the right direction when it comes to other people's love lives."

"Call it what you want, but we both know what you're doing," Grace said with a slight smile.

"How's the investigation going so far?" Jake asked me.

"Why don't we talk about it later?" I suggested. "Here's our food."

The tray went to the table behind us though, and my disappointment must have shown on my face. Antonia winked at me and grinned. "Don't worry, yours is coming right up."

"I hope so," I said with a smile of my own. "I'm sitting here wasting away to nothing." It couldn't be farther from the truth. I was carrying a good fifteen pounds more than I needed, and Antonia was whisper thin, but at that moment, seeing the food and smelling the delightful aromas all around me was almost too much for me to take.

As promised, she was back in less than a minute with our food. I had ordered ravioli, Jake the spaghetti and meatballs, while Grace got the baked ziti. "I have an idea," I said. "Let's split all three meals. They look so good, I'd love a little bit of each. What do you all say? Are you up for it?"

Grace grinned and nodded as Jake asked, "Why not?"

We were divvying up the food as Angelica came over to our table, frowning. "Is something wrong?"

"No, we just decided to split our meals three ways," I said.

Before I could stop her, she collected Grace's plate and then Jake's. After she turned to get mine, I held on to it tightly. "Angelica, you know that I love you, but I don't think so."

"Suzanne, let me take these back into the kitchen and do this right," she insisted.

"Okay," I agreed reluctantly. It was tough seeing my food disappear, but it was all quickly returned, divided neatly and evenly.

"Isn't that better?" she asked as she served us again.

"It looks wonderful."

"It does, doesn't it?" Angelica asked. "Maybe we'll add a mix and match to our menu. Maria has been nagging me to jazz things up a bit, and this just might do it. Enjoy."

"We will, I'm certain of that," I said.

As we ate, the fire at ReNEWed and Gabby's condition didn't come up in the conversation. Instead, it was just a nice meal with two of the people I loved most in the world. As evenings went, it would be a tough one to top.

Angelica brought us the bill, which Jake and Grace fought over before my husband arose victorious, and she asked, "Have you heard about the robberies in town?"

"Have there been any more lately?" Jake asked her.

"There was one this morning as Melanie Anspic was opening her shop for the day. He wore a mask and had a gun, and he completely cleaned her out."

"What's the name of her business?" I asked.

"Melanie's Notions. He only got a few hundred dollars, but the poor woman is talking about shutting down altogether, she's so afraid he'll come back. I'm concerned that our new police chief is in over his head."

She glanced up as a man in uniform approached us. He was younger than Stephen Grant, and while our police chief had an air of confidence and competence about him, this young man appeared to be uncomfortable, in both his chief's uniform and his new role.

"What do you know? My mother used to say it all of the time: 'Speak of the devil, and he appears.' It's a ghastly quote, isn't it?" She turned to the chief. "Hello, Chief Erskine. Have you caught our robber yet?"

"We're following up on some promising leads," the man said as he motioned to Jake. "Inspector, could I have a minute of your time?"

Jake stayed put. "Sorry, but I haven't been an inspector in some time."

"Please?" the chief asked.

"Go on, Jake," I urged him.

He nodded as he put two twenties on the table. "I'll be right back."

As Angelica took the money to make change, Grace asked, "What was that all about?"

"The chief wants Jake to consult with him on these robberies. As a matter of fact, it was Stephen's idea in the first place."

Grace frowned. "He promised me that he wasn't going to try to get them together. I'm really sorry, Suzanne."

"Don't be," I said. "I think it might do Jake some good, and Chief Erskine clearly needs all of the help he can get. He looks a bit like a scared young colt, doesn't he?"

"Can you blame him? He's had the job less than three weeks, and there have already been four robberies in Union Square. Stephen tried to help him out, but he's got his hands full just dealing with April Springs. What do you think?"

"I think he needs to catch whoever is doing this before he loses his job," I said.

"I mean about Jake helping out," Grace persisted.

"Personally, I think it's a great idea," I said.

"Seriously? You wouldn't mind?" She seemed surprised by my statement, and it pleased me that I wasn't completely predictable, even to my best friend.

"It's what Jake was born to do, catching bad guys," I said. "I know he has some doubts about doing it on a permanent basis again, but I think this would be perfect. He can consult with police forces around here when they need him and still do things like helping the mayor with his remodeling project. It's the best of both worlds, if you ask me."

"I can't believe you haven't suggested it to him," Grace said.

"I have, but tonight we're going to have a much more serious conversation about it. Do me a favor."

"Anything," Grace said. "All you have to do is ask."

"When Jake gets back, don't say anything about it. I want to hit him at home when he's least expecting it."

"You're a devious woman and a conniving wife, Suzanne Hart," Grace said with a smile. "Someday I want to grow up to be just like you."

I had to laugh. Maybe I *was* being a little sneaky, but it was for my husband's own good, and after all, his happiness was paramount to me.

When he returned to the table, Angelica had already made change. "I took care of the tip," I said.

"You didn't have to," Jake protested.

"I didn't. It was out of your change. By the way, you were feeling *very* generous tonight."

He laughed. "You know me. I'm just that kind of guy. Are you ladies ready to get out of here?"

"Let's go," I said.

Once we were outside, I told my husband, "I could ride home with you if Grace drives my Jeep."

"Okay," Grace said hesitantly. I knew she didn't really like driving it, but if I rode back to April Springs with Jake, it would give us a chance to talk about him consulting with Chief Erskine, and I wouldn't have to wait until we got home.

"Don't be crazy," Jake said, vetoing the idea instantly. "You two go on. I've got to swing by Hartman Building Supply while I'm in town anyway. They're open till nine, and George wanted me to check out a new oscillating saw they just got in. I'll give him credit. That man's not afraid to spend money on new tools."

"So, he's a guy after your own heart," I said with a smile.

"Hey, I don't buy anything I don't need," Jake protested.

"Of course not," I agreed quickly. "Why would you?"

He looked a little uneasy about winning so effortlessly, but I was just setting him up for the conversation we were going to have later at home. "Drive safe."

"You, too," he said.

After I collected a quick kiss, he went off to the hardware store, and Grace and I got into my Jeep. "Where to?" I asked her.

"Well, we've just about exhausted our suspects here in town," Grace said. "Should we head back to April Springs and see how Gabby's doing?"

"That's an excellent idea," I said as I started the Jeep and we took off. It had been an hour since I'd thought about my friend's condition, and I felt bad about it. After all, while she was fighting for her life, I'd been enjoying a night out with my best friend and my husband.

As we headed back to town, I found myself hoping that Gabby's tenacity would prove to be the thing that saved her. Somehow I couldn't bear the thought of having a Gabby-sized hole in my life. It would be hard enough not having ReNEWed right beside me. Her shop had been a fixture in April Springs long before I'd opened Donut

Hearts, and as Gabby had often liked to say, it would be there long after I was gone.

It turned out that she had been very wrong about that indeed.

Chapter 13

"So, what do you think of the case so far?" I asked Grace as we drove back in the general direction of home. "Is it at all possible that the fire was an accident?"

"Not knowing Gabby," Grace said. "I've got the feeling that whoever set that fire didn't know Gabby all that well. Did you even know that she had a toaster oven in the shop?"

"No, as a matter of fact, I didn't," I said. "Is it possible that whoever did it brought it with them?"

"I doubt that, but I wonder what else was near it? Maybe Gabby was putting together a donation for Goodwill. Isn't that how she discarded clothes she couldn't sell?"

"That's true enough. Okay, let's say she brought it from home to take in with her other donations, and after she was struck down from behind, whoever did it panicked and looked around for a reason to set a fire to cover their tracks. It wouldn't be hard to fray a cord and plug it in after the fire was set. If we look at it that way, it makes sense."

"At least more sense than Gabby plugging it in herself," I said. A sudden thought occurred to me, and I wondered why I hadn't thought of it before. "Grace, we need to call Stephen right now."

"And say what?" she asked as she pulled out her cell phone.

"If we're right and someone set that fire to cover up their assault on Gabby, they have to make sure that she *never* regains consciousness,"

I said. "That puts her life in danger every second she can't tell anyone what really happened."

"I'll call him," Grace said, "and I'll put it on speaker, too."

"Hey," the chief answered on the third ring. "What's up?"

"Do you have anybody guarding Gabby at the hospital?" Grace asked him.

"No, of course not. I can't spare that kind of manpower," the chief said. "Besides, the fire was set by accident. There's no reason in the world to believe that Gabby's in any danger."

"Chief, it's Suzanne," I interjected. "What if you're wrong?"

"I still can't spare someone around the clock to keep an eye on her," the chief said, "but I don't think I'm wrong."

"Can't you at least have someone swing by and check on her every now and then?" Grace asked.

I knew that would be useless even as she asked the question. If someone really wanted to kill her, they'd just wait until the moment was right and strike when no one was watching.

"I suppose I could do that," he said. "The last I heard, she was still in ICU. She'd be tough to get to there. They watch them around the clock."

I let out a sigh of relief. "Then we should be all right, at least for now."

"Ladies, far be it from me to criticize either one of your sleuthing skills, but I think you're seeing things that aren't there this time."

"Thanks for the advice," I said as I motioned to Grace with a cutting motion.

"Gotta go. Talk to you soon," she said, hanging up before he had a chance to ask us what we'd been up to. "Well, that turned out to be a wash," Grace said as she put her phone away.

"Don't stick that phone back in your bag so fast. I want to talk to Chief Lane."

"What do you think the fire chief can tell us that we don't already know?" she asked me.

"I'm not sure, but why don't we call him, and we'll find out," I suggested.

She had to look the number up, and the fire chief answered on the second ring. "Hello?"

"Chief, this is Suzanne Hart and Grace Gauge," I said. "We were wondering if we could ask you something about the fire at ReNEWed."

He paused a long time before answering, and when he did, there was a definite weariness in his voice. "So, you think it was deliberately set, too, don't you?"

"We do, but why do you think so?" Grace asked him.

"I've been in this line of work for a very long time. There was something about it that just wasn't right," he said. "It was all a little too convenient, if you know what I mean."

"We don't, actually," Grace said.

"I keep going over it again and again, and that toaster oven should never have been plugged in where it was."

"Where exactly was it? Did there happen to be anything else around it?" I asked him.

"It was in the middle of several boxes of clothes, at least I think it was. I didn't exactly have a lot of time to study the scene, if you know what I mean. I was too busy checking on Gabby and then trying to get her out of there."

"Did you happen to notice if there were any *other* small kitchen appliances nearby?" I asked him.

He clucked his tongue a bit. "How in the world did you know that? I stumbled over a blender and a beat-up old mixer that were on the floor, too."

So maybe our theory had been right after all. If Gabby had been doing some cleaning at home and was putting together a donation, the toaster oven would make sense being in the shop. "Did you tell the inspector what you saw?"

"I tried to, but he kind of dismissed me out of hand. I got the distinct impression that he thought I was a doddering old fool too antiquated to still be on the job." He said it with a hint of bitterness in his voice, and really, I couldn't blame him. It was an awful thing to be discounted just because of his age. Whatever happened to valuing experience?

"You carried her out of that fire, and I doubt the inspector could have done that," I said. "You should be proud of what you did."

"Thanks, Suzanne," he said. "I appreciate that. I don't know. Maybe he's right. It could be time for me to hang it up. I'm still having trouble bouncing back after what happened. My body just isn't the same as it used to be."

"How could it be?" Grace asked him. "I'll tell you something, Chief. If *I'm* ever in a burning building, I hope you're around to carry me out."

"Let's hope it never comes to that, as much as I appreciate the sentiment."

"The inspector didn't find any direct evidence of an accelerant, but he didn't have his dog with him, so he could be wrong," I said.

"Not every arson case has to use gasoline or kerosene," the chief said. "There was enough flammable material in that shop that whoever set it might not have needed it. That's the problem with science some of the time. Common sense seems to go out the window."

"Are you going to pursue your theory?" I asked the chief.

"I could appeal it, but until and unless Gabby comes to and tells us what really happened, it wouldn't do much good. There's just too much work as it is for too few people. I really hope she makes it," he added almost wistfully.

"So do we," I said. "We're heading over there right now to check on her."

"Let me know how she's doing," Chief Lane said, "and if she happens to wake up, tell her I said hello."

"*When* she wakes up, you mean," I said, stressing the word "when," "I'm sure you're the first person she'll want to talk to. She'll want to thank you for being so heroic."

"I was just doing my job," he said, but I could hear a hint of pride in his voice.

"And doing it rather well at that," Grace said.

"Thanks, ladies. You do an old fire chief good."

"Thank *you*, Chief," we said nearly in unison, and then, as we were all laughing, we ended the call.

"What do you think?" Grace asked me.

"I think we'd better solve this before Gabby gets out of ICU," I said. "Once she's in a regular room and not being monitored around the clock, I have a hunch that whoever tried to get rid of her will make another go of it."

"Let's talk about our suspects again," I said. We still had a ways to go before we got to the hospital, and we might as well use the time productively.

"Sounds good," Grace said. "Buster Breckinridge has to be at the top of our list."

"He had motive enough, and any one of our suspects would have the means, but did he have the opportunity?" I asked her.

"Don't forget the dinner break he and Manny took separately," Grace reminded me.

"I was just about to mention that," I said. "Either one of them could have done it, and Manny had his own motive if Gabby was making things difficult for him, which we both know she was more than capable of doing."

"Okay, how about Tyra Hitchings?" Grace asked me.

"She admitted herself that she had an argument with Gabby, but it's hard to believe that she'd kill her over feeling cheated on her prices,"

I said. "Then again, we both know how proud Tyra is, and she's certainly got a temper. She could have lashed out, and not just verbally, and then tried to cover her tracks, especially if she thought Gabby was already dead."

"That has to go for Mindy Fulbright, too," Grace added. "If she felt that Gabby was stealing her man, she could have lashed out in anger, or even a fit of jealousy."

"I know it's hard to see Mindy in that light," I said reluctantly, "but I have to agree with you there. After all, we've both seen people do worse things in the name of love than that in the past. She has to stay on our list."

"Wow, who knew Gabby had that many people who would want to see the end of her?" Grace asked, and then she quickly corrected herself. "Fine, I know that she's not the most popular person in town, but burning her shop down after assaulting her goes way beyond the usual scope of things."

"I can't believe it was planned," I said. "Everything about it says that it was spur of the moment. How would someone possibly know there would be something in the shop they could blame the fire on? Besides, it appears that Gabby was struck down from behind, not something that would probably be planned out ahead of time. We need to get a feel for who would act impulsively in the situation."

"Funny, but looking at it from that perspective, it almost feels as though Buster is the *only* one we should discount," Grace said.

"Why do you say that?"

"He was in prison for what must have felt like an eternity to him," she said. "Wouldn't you think if he really wanted revenge for Gabby's testimony, he could have come up with something better than bashing her in the back of the head and then setting ReNEWed on fire? If he burned the shop down, he had to know that the police would come looking for him first, especially since he has a history of arson, no matter what he might claim. A fire is the absolute worst thing he could do."

"Unless he was being a little *too* cute," I said. "He might consider setting a blaze poetic justice."

We both looked at each other for a moment and then shook our heads at the same time. "No," I said, "I don't think he's that clever."

"Still, he needs to stay on the list, just maybe not at the top of it," Grace said.

"Agreed."

As we neared the hospital, I felt myself tense up. I couldn't imagine what Gabby's state was at the moment. She could have recovered from the blow *and* the fire, or she could have succumbed to the assault.

Until I heard otherwise though, I would keep digging into what had happened at ReNEWed with Grace.

I owed that to my friend, at the very least.

Chapter 14

When we got there, Gabby wasn't in the intensive care unit. "What's going on, Penny?" I asked as I saw my friend at the nurses station.

"Don't look so panicked! She's still alive, Suzanne," she said quickly. "They moved her to a private room."

"Is she awake?" I asked her as relief flooded through me.

"She is, and her improvement is amazing. As a matter of fact, I was just about to call you. She's demanding to see you."

"Why? Did she say what she wanted?" I asked.

"She didn't say a word to me, but you know she's good friends with the hospital administrator, so we're all doing our best to be as pleasant to her as possible." In a lower voice, she added, "You can imagine how challenging that can be, given the circumstances."

I knew exactly what she meant. Gabby could be bristly on her best days, and this was certainly not one of those.

"She didn't ask for me too, did she?" Grace asked, clearly hoping that the summons had been meant just for me.

"Your name came up as well," Penny said with a grin. "She's in 214."

"Thanks," I said.

"Good luck," she added as we walked down the hallway toward the elevator.

I turned around and gave her a thumbs-up, though I didn't feel all that confident about my ability to handle the situation. I had to wonder what Gabby would say when we showed up, but there was no point speculating.

In a minute we'd find out what had happened directly from her.

Or so I thought.

"Suzanne, where have you been?" were the first words out of Gabby's mouth the moment we walked through the door. "I've been asking for you for the last thirty minutes."

"As flattering as that is, why me?" I asked her.

Instead of answering, she turned to Grace. "Hello, Grace. Thanks for coming with Suzanne."

"You know us. We're a matched set," she said. "How are you feeling, Gabby?"

Gabby gently touched the padded bandage on the back of her head and sighed. "I've got a headache you wouldn't believe, I'm having a little trouble breathing, and to top it all off, they won't let me get out of bed without an escort. Besides that, I couldn't be better," she added with more than a hint of sarcasm in her voice.

"Gabby, I'm so glad you're alive," I said as I touched her hand lightly. I was half afraid she'd recoil from my touch, but instead, she put her free hand over mine.

"That makes two of us. Listen, I desperately need your help."

"We'll do whatever we can," I said. "What's going on? Tell us what happened at the shop."

She pulled her hands away, and the look of anguish on her face was tough to see. "That's the thing. I don't remember."

"What part of it don't you recall?" I asked her.

"I don't remember *any* of it," Gabby confessed. "Our esteemed police chief just left, and he was having a difficult time believing that I wasn't holding out on him. He thought I might be protecting someone! How insane is that? Why would I protect someone who tried to kill me?"

"So, it wasn't an accident?" I asked her.

"No, of course it wasn't. I don't remember exactly what happened, but I *never* would have plugged that toaster oven in, especially in my shop. I was putting together a bunch of things from the house and the shop so I could make a donation. That blasted thing has a short in the cord, so I had a note on it saying not to use it until it was repaired, that it was a fire hazard. How prophetic that turned out to be."

So we'd been right in our speculations after all. "I don't know if anyone has told you yet, but ReNEWed is gone," I said. I was a firm believer that bad news was best delivered quickly and without fanfare.

"So I heard," she said, dismissing it as though I'd told her that it was raining outside. "I had insurance, so I should be fine."

"Are you going to rebuild the shop?" Grace asked her.

"I have no idea. At the moment, I have more pressing concerns. I need you two to find out who tried to kill me, and why."

"That's kind of what we've been doing since the fire," I admitted.

That brought a smile to Gabby's face. "Good girls. I knew you wouldn't take this lying down."

"What exactly *do* you remember?" Grace asked her.

"The last thing I can recall is opening the shop yesterday morning. It was business as usual, and the next thing I knew, I was waking up in ICU! I've got to tell you, I just about had a heart attack."

"Did the chief fill you in on what's been happening in the meantime?" I asked her.

"He was about to, but then he was called away for an emergency. As if what I'm going through right now doesn't count as an emergency, too." She paused, took a sip of water, and then asked, "What do you have so far?"

"We have some suspects," I admitted. "Listen, it's not going to be easy for you to hear what we've uncovered. Are you sure you're feeling good enough to go through this?"

"I need to know, Suzanne," she said firmly. "Good, bad, or indifferent, it's vital that we figure out what really happened."

"Okay. Here's what we've got so far. Our list of suspects at the moment is: Buster Breckinridge, Tyra Hitchings, Mindy Fulbright, and Manny Wright."

She didn't look surprised to hear any of the names except Buster's. "That pyromaniac's back in town the day my shop burns to the ground? Why isn't he in jail?"

"He's got an alibi, of sorts," I told her. "He works for Manny at the Garden Center in Union Square, and they kind of cover for each other."

"But?" Gabby asked.

"There's a large enough gap in time where they were apart, so it doesn't hold together."

"Okay. I remember a nice evening with Manny three days ago, or four or five I suppose, since apparently I've lost a few days along the way. Why would *he* want to kill me?"

Now she was going to have to hear the news that he was a scoundrel all over again. I didn't relish it, and I was still trying to figure out a way to tell her when Grace spoke up. "Evidently he's been using the Internet to troll for lots and lots of women of a certain age, though he's promised them all they were exclusive."

Gabby frowned for a moment, but then she fought it back and shrugged. "I should have known that he was too good to be true. Let me guess. He was also wooing Tyra and Mindy, is that right?"

"Not Tyra, at least not that we know of yet," I said. "That's on our list of questions to ask her the next time we see her."

"Then why would she want to see me dead?"

"The theory is that she came into the store and found out what you were charging for her things," Grace said. "We have an eyewitness who claims Tyra stormed out of the shop not that long before the fire started."

"I'm a businesswoman," Gabby said, "or at least I was. I deserve to make a profit, or why else bother?"

"Evidently she had an issue with the size of your margins," Grace said with a half smile.

"Nobody held a gun to her head and made her sell me those things," Gabby said. "She was certainly under no obligation to do business with me. The woman didn't even dicker over what I offered to pay her, if you can believe that! Of course I lowballed her." Gabby seemed to chew on all that we'd told her for a few moments.

While she was thinking, I had something I needed to say. "Gabby, we're working on the theory that whoever set that fire did so to cover up killing you."

"I'm not dead, though," Gabby protested, quite rightly, too.

"They obviously didn't know that at the time," I amended. "We believe that the arsonist hit you from behind in a fit of rage, and then, thinking you were dead, decided to cover up the crime. It's not the first time it's been done," I said, thinking about our flip house project and what had happened to it, all in order to hide the facts. "Chances are whoever did it doesn't know you've lost your memory of what happened. Has the doctor said anything about how long it will last?"

"It could come back to me at any second," Gabby admitted. "Then again, I may never remember what happened."

"The arsonist doesn't know that, though. You're not safe here," Grace said.

"Before you ask, we've already asked the police chief to post someone on your door, but he claims he doesn't have the manpower unless the threat can be substantiated," I added.

"I'm not his favorite person in the world," Gabby admitted.

"Hang on a second," Grace said, rising to her boyfriend's defense. "I'm sure that never even entered his mind. They've lost two officers in the past month, and he's having a difficult time finding replacements. Chief Grant is stretched so thin that he's even started taking shifts patrolling again himself. It's not fair to assume that he's not protecting you out of spite."

Gabby surprised me by being the one who was calm. "Take it easy, Grace. I know you're right." She thought for a few moments, and then she said, "I need to make a phone call."

I handed her my phone. "Who are you calling?"

She ignored my request for information. "Jessie? It's Gabby. The room is fine. I need a favor. Would it be okay if my nephew puts a chair outside my room and keeps an eye on things? I'd rather not say. How about forty-eight? Okay then, thirty-six. Good. Thanks."

"You're getting your own guard," I said. "I didn't even know you had a nephew."

"Technically he's a cousin, but I doubted Jessie would go for that, so I bumped him up in status," Gabby said as she dialed another number.

"Bo, it's Gabby. Yes, I'm awake. I need to see you. Of course I'm still at the hospital. No, tomorrow won't do. Be here in half an hour."

"Are you sure he's up to the task?" I asked her after the call ended.

"He's not a cop, but he used to play high school football, and he's a scary-looking brute with a full bushy beard and tattoos up and down his arms. I doubt anybody's going to try anything with him outside. I could only buy you thirty-six hours, though. Do you think you can solve this in that amount of time?"

"We'll do everything in our power," I said. "Is there anything you can tell us that might help? Anything at all?"

"I'm at a loss," Gabby admitted. "I don't have to tell you that I've never been the most popular girl in school, not like you, Grace, or someone with hundreds of friends, like you, Suzanne." We both tried to protest, but she raised a hand. "I'm too tired and too sore and too old to listen to your protests. My point is that while I know a great many folks in April Springs don't care for me, I don't know of anyone who would actually want to see me dead."

"Is that just in April Springs?" Grace asked with a glint in her eye. "How about outside the town limits?"

It was a risky time to joke, and I would have warned her not to do it if I'd known what she was about to say, but Gabby took it with a smile after a few moments of hesitation. "True enough, but let's focus on folks in the immediate area for now, shall we?"

"We shall," Grace said.

As we got up to leave, Gabby asked, "Grace, would you give us a minute?"

"Of course," Grace said. "I sincerely hope you're feeling better. We were worried about you."

"Just knowing that you two are helping is making me feel as though I'm on the mend already," she said with one of her rare smiles.

After Grace was gone, I asked, "What is it?"

"I may have misjudged that girl," Gabby said, reflecting on Grace for a moment.

"I think so, but that isn't what this is about, is it?"

Gabby shook her head. "No, I suppose not. Suzanne, if Buster did this to me, he could be after you, too. Have you considered that possibility? It's not all that hard to believe that he would try to burn both of us out of business with one match, or more specifically, one toaster oven. You need to watch your back, do you hear me?"

"I'm being as careful as I can be," I said, touched by Gabby's concern for my welfare.

"I understand that, but you're making a target of yourself by going around snooping into other people's lives, and if anything happened to you because you were doing something I asked you to do, I'd never be able to forgive myself."

I patted her hand lightly. "Gabby, we were already working on this even before you asked us to do anything. Grace and I are determined to find out what happened to you, and ReNEWed. If anything should happen to either one of us, which I'm sure it won't, it won't be on your head, okay?"

"Okay," she said reluctantly.

"Should we stick around until Bo shows up?" I asked.

"Oh, he'll be here soon, I'm sure of it," Gabby said.

"Fine. We'll keep in touch, and if you remember anything, no matter how trivial it might seem to you, tell us immediately, okay?"

"I will," she said. "Now run along and find out who did this, Suzanne."

"We'll do our very best," I promised.

Chapter 15

I found Grace out in front of Gabby's room, sitting in a chair that someone must have already provided.

"Wow, Jessie Hassop doesn't waste any time, does she?"

"The administrator didn't do this," Grace said. "I asked Penny for a chair, and she got this one for me. Suzanne, should we just leave Gabby unguarded until Bo gets here? I don't feel right about it."

"Neither do I," I said with a grin. "I was about to suggest the same thing. Let's hang around until he shows up."

We didn't have long to wait. Less than ten minutes later, a hulking young man with flowing black hair and a bushy beard approached us. He had sleeves of tattoos on both arms, and I had no doubt this was the infamous Bo we'd been waiting for. There was a well-worn canvas messenger bag tucked under one arm that looked as though it belonged to a child, it was so small by comparison to the man who carried it.

"You must be Bo," I said as I offered my hand.

His grip swallowed mine, but I was surprised to find that his touch was delicate and quite gentle. "Guilty as sin," he said with a bright grin. "You've got to be Suzanne, and that would make you Grace," he said as he nodded to each of us in turn. "Thanks for looking out for Gabby. She's just about all I've got left in the world since my folks died. She's quite an old gal, isn't she?" He said it with such obvious affection that I could tell that the two of them had a special bond. "Is there anything in particular I'm supposed to be watching out for?"

"If anyone, and I mean anyone, goes into her room, keep an eye on them while they're in there," I said. "If everything goes well, I'm afraid you're going to be bored to tears for the next thirty-six hours. At least that's what I'm hoping for."

"Don't worry about me," Bo said. "I've got a poem I've been working on for ages that's been giving me fits. I can't tell you how much trouble I'm having composing in iambic pentameter."

"You're a poet?" Grace asked him, clearly as startled as I was by the news.

His grin lit up his entire face. "I know, I don't fit the mold of what most people think a poet should look like, but what can I say? When I blew out my knee playing football in college, I had to find something else to do with my life, and literature found me. As for me being a poet, all I can say is that I'm an aspiring one, which is about as useless as a buggy whip manufacturer these days, but what can I say? It's my passion."

Clearly this man had a great many layers.

"You're going to need to take breaks every now and then," I said. "Should we try to get you some reinforcements?"

"Thanks, but I have a few friends who have already agreed to pitch in," he said with a grin. "They're all pretty scary looking, but every last one of them has a good heart. Trust me, nobody's going to mess with Gabby while we're on watch."

I couldn't imagine who *Bo* might describe as scary, given his own general appearance. It was funny how I'd judged him unfairly on his appearance the moment I'd first seen him. If we'd been speaking on the phone, I would have thought I was talking to a refined young man with intelligence and self-deprecation, not the tattooed giant before me. I liked this young man, and I was happy that Gabby had him in her life. "After this is all over, come by Donut Hearts, and I'll treat you to some goodies," I said.

"Thanks, but I've got a gluten allergy," he said with a sigh.

"I've got a few that are gluten free on the menu every day," I said.

"Then I'll take you up on your offer," he said with a smile. "Let me pop in and tell Gabby that I'm here. Thanks again for looking out for her. She's talked about you two a lot in the past, so I know that she trusts you both completely."

It surprised me to learn that Gabby had talked about us both to anyone, let alone in glowing terms, but I was going to take it with a smile. "We'll do our best to make this all go away."

"If you can, I'll owe you both, and that's not something I say lightly," Bo said seriously.

"We're doing it because we care about her, too," I said.

"I know that. That's why I made the offer," Bo said. He saluted us both and then walked into his cousin's room.

"Well, Gabby certainly seems to be in good hands," Grace said as we walked out to the Jeep and headed back into the heart of downtown. "He's an interesting fellow, isn't he?"

"I like him," I said with a smile.

"Me, too," Grace replied. "I know we don't have a lot of time left before you have to go to bed. Is there anything you want to do tonight, or should we stop now and get busy tomorrow after you close the donut shop for the day?"

"We don't have to wait that long," I told her. "Tomorrow is Emma and Sharon's turn to run the shop. I'm free if you are."

Grace coughed a moment as she grinned at me. "You know, I may be coming down with something, Suzanne. It might be a good idea for me to take a sick day off from work."

"Only if you can afford to lose one," I said.

"Are you kidding? I *never* use all of the days I get. How early should we start? Bear in mind that I'm not used to getting up at the crack of 2:30 in the morning, and neither will anyone we need to speak with."

"Let's have breakfast at the Boxcar at seven a.m.," I said. "Is that still early for you?"

"No, seven I can make happen," she said with a smile. "Does that mean that we're finished for the night?"

I thought about how much time we had left, and how much energy I had. After all, I'd spent a long day making donuts, and then we'd chased clues down across two towns before having a pretty emotional reunion with Gabby. "I could probably squeeze one more interview in before we call it a night," I said as I stifled a yawn. "Who would you like to talk to?"

"Forget I said anything," Grace answered with a grin. "If I'm laying out tomorrow, there are things I need to do in the meantime. Let's go home, and we can get a fresh start tomorrow. How does that sound?"

"It sounds good to me," I said. "I still need to talk to Jake."

"Are you going to be all right?" Grace asked me. "I'm willing to be your sounding board, if you need one."

"Thanks, but I don't want to lose my nerve by talking about it with you before I share my thoughts with him," I said.

"You'll tell me what happened tomorrow though, right?" she asked me with a grin.

"You know I will," I said as I stopped in her driveway long enough to drop her off. As we'd driven past what had once been ReNEWed, I found myself still having a hard time believing that Gabby's shop was gone. How long would it be before I looked at the space beside Donut Hearts and didn't see it still there, or at least a ghostly memory of it?

"I'll see you in the morning," Grace said. "Good luck."

I was happy to see Jake's truck parked in front of the cottage when I got there. The last thing I wanted to do when I got home was to have to wait around for my husband to show up, but he was sitting on the couch waiting for me as soon as I walked through the door.

Before I could say a word though, he beat me to it. "Suzanne, we need to talk."

I had a feeling that I wasn't going to like what he had to say, based on his tone of voice and body language.

What on earth was my husband about to tell me?

"What's going on?" I asked him as I sat down on the chair across from him.

"I've got something to talk to you about, and I'd appreciate it if you'd hear me out without saying anything until I'm finished."

He looked so serious. "I can do that," I promised.

"I spoke with Chief Erskine again this evening, and I'm going to take the consulting job he's offered me."

I started to speak despite my promise, but one look at Jake and I knew I had to let him say what he had to say. "Suzanne, I've given this a lot of thought, and it's something I want to do. I know I've taken a stab or two at consulting in the past, and I'm not sure I want to do this on a permanent basis, but for the moment, it feels like the right time for me to dip a toe back into the water. We both know that I've missed being in law enforcement, and this just might be the best of both worlds. At least for this job I won't be gone from home at night, and I still get to do what I love. I've kept saying no because I know how you feel about me putting my life in danger again, but I can't live the rest of my life covered in bubble wrap. If I'm not taking chances every now and then, I don't feel as though I'm even alive. I'm not one hundred percent certain that this is for me, but for now, at least for this case, it's what I want to do. After that, we'll play it by ear and see what happens." He clearly felt better getting all of that off his chest, but I wasn't about to speak until he asked me for my opinion. "Don't worry about me putting George on hold with the remodeling project. He's running low on money for the next supplies we need, and besides, I think he'd like to take a break. This shouldn't take long, and by the time I help Chief Erskine wrap this case up, he'll be ready to get back to work again." Jake looked at me expectantly, but I wasn't about to say anything until I was invited to comment. "Well? What do you think?"

"I think it's amazing," I said. "I don't know why you didn't think I'd be all for it. After all, I get to do what I love to do. Why shouldn't you?"

"I know you've said that in the past, but I also know that you worry about me," Jake said.

"Of course I do," I said. "You worry about me too, don't you?"

"You know I do, but I'd never keep you from making donuts, or digging into murder either, for that matter."

"Or even attempted murder and arson?" I asked.

"So, you still believe the fire at Gabby's place was deliberate?"

"I know it was," I said. "I've got to catch you up on quite a few things. Do you have the time, or are you going to start working tonight?"

He laughed. "No, first thing in the morning will be soon enough." After a momentary pause, he added, "Unless you need me for your investigation. Then I can tell Chief Erskine no."

"Thanks for the offer, but working with me and working with the police in an official capacity are two different things, and we both know it. Besides, I've got Grace."

"Yes, you do. So, bring me up to speed on what's been happening."

It was clear that he felt relieved having gotten through the conversation with me. I couldn't understand why he'd been worried. We communicated better than just about any other married couple I knew, but there were still times when we got things wrong. It just proved that we needed to keep talking, to keep working on our relationship, no matter how good it might be.

"First of all, Gabby's awake," I said.

He looked startled. "Since when? Why didn't you tell me?"

"I was about to, but you had your speech all ready, and you weren't about to be interrupted," I said with a grin.

"Sorry about that," Jake apologized.

"You have nothing to be sorry about," I said. "Gabby's doing much better, but there's a problem. She's lost her recent memory, so she has no idea who hit her, or who started the fire."

Jake didn't look all that surprised. "It happens more often than you might think. Sudden trauma like that can really rattle your brain. If she doesn't remember anything, how is she so sure she didn't start the fire herself?"

"That toaster oven was defective, and she knew it. She was going to donate it, along with a few other things. They would fix it, that's part of what they do, but she put a note on it saying that it was a fire hazard, and Chief Lane thinks he saw it sitting beside several boxes of clothes when he rescued Gabby from the shop."

"He *thinks*?" Jake asked.

"That's what he told us, but as he said, he was kind of busy at the time saving Gabby's life," I replied.

"So, who are your suspects? Do you have motives for them? How about alibis?" Jake was clearly gearing up for being in full-on investigative mode, and I knew that Chief Erskine of Union Square was going to get more than he was hoping for in my husband. Jake had some serious credentials when it came to solving crime; there was no doubt about that.

"Buster Breckinridge has got to be right up there. He had reason to hate Gabby and me because of our testimonies in court," I said. "He could have thought that burning ReNEWed down would also take out Donut Hearts too, which wasn't far from being the truth. He claims to have been working for Manny Wright at the time, another of our suspects, but there are holes in both their alibis. Manny has been dating several women in the area, supposedly all exclusively, and Gabby was one of them. Another one was Mindy Fulbright, who evidently had a fight with her over the man, though Gabby doesn't remember any of it. Finally, we've got Tyra Hitchings. She's got a temper, and she found out how much Gabby was profiting off of the things she'd been selling to her, and they had words about it soon before the fire. We don't have alibis for the ladies yet, so that's right up at the top of our list of things to do tomorrow morning."

"That's right, it's Emma and Sharon's day at the donut shop," Jake said. "Will Grace be able to get off work to help you with the investigation?"

"She's calling in sick," I said with a grin.

"Okay then, I won't worry about you. When are you two meeting? Any chance you'll have time to have breakfast with me before you get started?"

I bit my lower lip. "Sorry, but Grace and I are meeting at the Boxcar Grill at seven," I said. "You're more than welcome to join us."

"As much as I love being a part of the Three Musketeers, I think I'll pass," Jake said. "Besides, I should probably get to Union Square early. I want to go over the files Erskine has on the robberies so far."

"Do you think it's one man?" I asked him.

"I'd be surprised if it weren't," Jake admitted. "One person, anyway. Suzanne, crime doesn't have any gender requirements. It might just be a woman."

"You're right, I should have said one person, but I know that better than most," I said. "Aren't armed robberies usually committed by men, though?"

"Usually," Jake allowed, "but certainly not always. Anyway, I need to dig into it before I even know enough to have an opinion." He stood and stretched. "I'm glad we cleared that up."

"Before we call it a day, do you have any tips for us in our interviews and investigation tomorrow?" I asked him. I wasn't above taking help wherever I could get it, especially from my husband. His years of experience in law enforcement were worth a great deal to me, and his insights were almost always on point.

"I'm sure you and Grace can handle it," he said. "I'm worried about Gabby, though. If you two are right, and someone attacked her and then set that fire, she's not safe."

"We've got that covered," I said. "Her cousin Bo and his friends are standing guard around the clock in front of her room, at least for the next day and a half."

"Are they cops?"

"No, but they're truly big and scary guys," I said. "I doubt any of our suspects would risk anything with them around."

"So, you've got a tight deadline," he said. "Don't be afraid to push your suspects a little harder than you're usually comfortable doing. Sometimes you take it a little too easy on them."

"That's why I've got Grace," I said.

"I know, but there are times that she pushes too hard," he said with a frown.

"So, between the two of us, we're in perfect balance," I answered with a grin.

"It doesn't work that way," Jake replied. "Watch your backs, okay?"

"We will," I said.

"What does Chief Grant think about you two meddling in the situation?"

"That's what's so exasperating," I admitted. "He's taking the fire inspector's word that it was an accident, at least he was the last time I spoke with him, so he's given us the okay to do a little digging on our own."

"You need to cut him some slack, Suzanne," Jake said. "He's got a dozen things on his plate at the moment. It's a tough job, and I should know. I had it for a while, remember?"

"I'm not likely to forget," I said.

As we got ready for bed, Jake asked me, "Have you heard from your mother lately? How's Phillip doing?"

"She came by the donut shop on a mission of mercy for him. According to her, he's sore and cranky," I admitted. "Momma's got her hands full, too."

"She'll be able to handle him if anyone can," Jake answered. "Should I pop in and see him? I'm going to be tied up in Union Square for the next few days, but I might be able to chisel out a little time to pop in on him if she thinks it might help."

"I believe right now all that he wants is to be left alone."

"I can respect that. Let your mother know that I'm here if she needs me."

I kissed my husband good night and was thankful yet again for the first case that had brought him into my life. I didn't mean Patrick Blaine's murder; that had been a terrible thing, but it had brought us together, and for that I would be eternally grateful.

Chapter 16

For a split second, I was surprised when I woke up the next morning for the second time and Jake was already gone. When I'd woken up at 2:30, out of habit more than need, he'd been softly snoring beside me, and then, at six a.m., I'd felt his lips lightly brush my forehead as he said good-bye. When Jake was on a case, he was an early riser, though not as early as I usually was, but then again, no one in their right mind got up in the middle of the night without a very good reason.

I grabbed a quick shower and got dressed, and then I drove to the Boxcar Grill. Grace and I would need a car for our investigation today, and her employers frowned on her taking her company vehicle out on personal business, especially when she was supposedly sick at home.

Grace was already sitting at a table when I got to the Boxcar.

"You actually beat me here?" I asked her with surprise after I greeted Trish and made my way to the table.

"I've been getting up early in the morning and walking through the park," she admitted.

"Since when? I've never seen you do it," I said as I looked at the breakfast menu. I felt like pancakes, but the ones I'd gotten at the Blue Ridge Café with Autumn would be tough to beat, no matter how good Hilda's might be.

"I just started this morning," she admitted, "but I can see doing it every day."

"That sounds good," I said as I kept scanning the menu. Eggs? No, I didn't feel like them, or an omelet, either. I knew I could always get a BLT, but that didn't sound good to me, either. I certainly wasn't going to have oatmeal or cereal. I was perfectly capable of making those things for myself at home.

It took me a second to realize that Grace had been talking to me as I'd been debating what to eat.

"Earth to Suzanne. What are you thinking about?"

"Food, what else?" I asked. "What were you saying?"

"I asked you if you'd like to join me on my walk on your days off," she said.

"Sure, why not?" I couldn't imagine it lasting more than a few days, but even if it became part of my routine on my days off, I'd welcome it. Not only would I get to spend quality time with Grace, but it also might help me keep my weight in better check. I knew from experience that cutting back on my donut sampling wasn't going to work. To be fair, I *had* to try the things I made. How else could I sell them in good faith to my customers? At least that was the lie I told myself with every bite.

"It's a deal, then," Grace said with a smile. "Now, what sounds good? Waffles. I haven't had them in forever, and I hate getting my old waffle iron out of the closet. I dropped it the last time I used it and nearly broke my toe. How about you?"

I pushed my menu aside. "Waffles sound good to me, too." They did, as a matter of fact. They were close enough to pancakes without being them, and not eggy at all, at least not if they were done right. I was happy that particular dilemma was solved. Now I could focus on other matters, like who had struck Gabby from behind and left her for dead in a fire they'd started themselves.

After we ordered, Trish vanished into the kitchen, and a few minutes later, she was back with our food. After placing two large glasses of orange juice in front of us, she set down our plates absolutely hidden by large stacks of waffles resting on each.

"Maybe we should have split an order," I said as I looked down at the daunting meal, with bacon on the side of each plate as well, as though there was any risk that either one of us wasn't going to get enough to eat. I didn't know how I was going to manage a third of the food and still be able to function well enough to drive, let alone interview our suspects and track down clues.

"You can always take what you don't eat home with you," Trish said. "Are the three of us still on for lunch today?"

I'd forgotten all about my promise to her, but when I thought about it, hadn't we fulfilled my pledge the day before? After all, we'd all had lunch together then, so I just kind of assumed that had taken care of the obligation. I couldn't bring myself to say it, though. Trish looked so eager for it to happen that there was no way I was going to disappoint her. "You bet."

She lowered her voice. "Listen, I heard Gabby was awake, so if you get tied up, I'll be happy to take a rain check."

"Thanks, but I can't imagine us not being able to carve out at least a little time for you later." As I poured some syrup on top of the already buttered waffles, I added, "If I even have an appetite for the rest of the day after eating this."

"I have faith in you both," Trish said happily as she went up front to take the money from one of her customers.

Grace asked me softly, "Am I crazy, or did we not just have lunch together yesterday?"

"I know, but I didn't have the heart to say no to her. Do you?"

"No," she readily admitted. Looking at her plate with dread in her gaze, she added, "I know I walked this morning and everything, but I'm not afraid to admit that I'm in way over my head here."

"Eat what you can, and we'll take the rest with us," I said.

The waffles were amazing, laced with cinnamon and nutmeg, and I found myself eating more than I thought I possibly could.

"So, where do we start this morning?" Grace asked me after finishing a delicate bite. At the rate she was going, we'd be there all day.

"I was thinking we should go back to Union Square to the Garden Center," I admitted. "That way we can kill two birds with one stone."

"If we can get either one of them to speak with us, that is," Grace allowed. "Neither man seemed all that cooperative yesterday, and I can't imagine they'd be any better today. What's our angle going to be?"

"I thought it was pretty clear, given what's happened. Now that Gabby's awake, whoever tried to burn her out is going to be especially jumpy, so I say we press every last one of our suspects as hard as we dare. *We* know she's lost the memories she needs to name who did this to her, but *they* won't."

"Are we actually using Gabby as bait?" Grace asked me after taking another bite.

"I prefer to think of it as expediting our case," I said. "Besides, with Bo and his friends watching over her, she's in good hands."

"For now, anyway," she answered.

"Grace, I don't like it any more than you do, but what choice do we have? Whether we like it or not, by tomorrow night, Gabby is going to be on her own."

"I know. I just wish there was a better way of doing this," Grace allowed.

"I do, too," I said sympathetically. "Then again, if it were easy, anybody could do it."

By the time I was finished with my meal, there wasn't enough left to even bother taking, but I had no idea how I was going to eat anything else that day, let alone lunch. Trish dropped off our checks, and we each took our own. Grace and I had recently had a discussion about her grabbing every bill we got eating out, and I'd finally gotten her to agree to letting each of us pay for our own meals, with one notable exception. We were free to, and even expected to, buy each other meals on our respective birthdays, but that was it.

Once we paid Trish, we were walking out of the Boxcar when we nearly ran over one of our suspects hurrying inside.

I hadn't been sure where we should start our investigation, but fate had dropped someone right into our laps, and who were we to turn that down?

"Were you looking for us, Mindy?" I asked as I sidestepped to get out of her way.

"What? No. Why would I be looking for either one of you?"

"We thought it might be about Gabby. She came out of her coma. Did you hear?"

Mindy's face went ashen, but she recovered. "That's wonderful," she said, doing her best to make us believe it. "What did she say about the fire?"

"It's coming back to her slowly," Grace said. "By tonight she should know what happened at ReNEWed. In the meantime, the police are tracking down alibis for everyone involved from six to seven on the night of the fire. Have they spoken with you yet?"

She looked surprised by the question. "Me? Why would they care about me?"

"Come on, Mindy. You said it yourself. You and Gabby had an argument about Manny Wright not long before the fire. Why *wouldn't* they want to speak with you?"

"You do have an alibi, don't you?" I asked her as sweetly as I could manage.

"I don't really know how to answer that question. I was home making dinner."

"Alone?" Grace asked.

"If you must know, Manny was supposed to come over for a meal, but he cancelled on me at the last minute," she admitted. "We were going to sort things out after what I found out about him and Gabby, but he stood me up yet again. It was the last straw for me. That's when I texted him and told him I never wanted to see him again."

"Funny, but you left that part out before," I pointed out.

"I didn't want to admit how weak I was," she said softly.

"So your answer is no, then. You don't have an alibi," Grace said flatly.

I knew we were supposed to be pushing our suspects, but I felt a little bit of sympathy for Mindy. After all, she'd had a rough time of it after her husband had died, and Manny had taken advantage of her vulnerable state, as far as I was concerned. If that made me soft, then so be it. I knew the hard questions had to be asked, but I was just as happy to let Grace do it.

"As a matter of fact, I suppose I do have someone who can vouch for me," she said with a bit of hesitation in her voice.

"Who would that be?" I asked her.

"Jenny White," she said.

"*Jenny* is your alibi?" I asked her. Jenny White was one of my mother's friends. In fact, the women had dinner together once a month and had been doing it for more years than I could remember. "How do you know Jenny?"

"She's my next-door neighbor. After I texted Manny and told him that it was over, I realized that I didn't want to be alone, so I asked her to come over and have dinner with me," Mindy said, and then she frowned. "I'm afraid that's not going to help me with the police, though."

"Why is that?"

"Didn't you know? Jenny is on some kind of a retreat. It's a spiritual thing, as far as I could tell. There are no phones there, no way to contact her at all for the next six weeks, so I guess I can't prove it after all, at least not right away."

Mindy paused, and then she looked around. A few folks were watching us, curious about our conversation no doubt. It was fair game in April Springs, where gossip and rumor were never far from the daily activities.

"Listen, I'm starving, so if you'll excuse me, I'm going to go in and have breakfast." Almost as an afterthought, she added, "That's great news about Gabby. Thanks for letting me know. As soon as I get the chance, I'm going to go apologize to her. Boy, I'm not looking forward to that particular conversation, as much as I need to have it."

"Do you believe her?" Grace asked me evenly after Mindy was gone.

"I don't know," I admitted. "It all makes perfect sense, but it could also be just a little *too* convenient that Jenny is out of town for the foreseeable future. There's no way to confirm or deny her alibi."

"In a way though, it lends some credence to her story, as far as I'm concerned," Grace said.

"What? Are you saying that you actually believe her?"

"Suzanne, if you were going to come up with an alibi, would you make one up that couldn't be confirmed for weeks and weeks? It would have almost been better if she hadn't had one at all."

"Now who's the one who's going soft?" I asked her with a smile.

"Maybe there's nothing wrong with thinking the best of the people we live with in April Springs," Grace admitted.

"I couldn't agree with you more," I said as I reached for my cell phone. "I need to make a quick call."

"Are you calling Jake?" she asked me.

"No, Momma."

"Hey, Momma, do you have a second?" I asked after she picked up.

"I do, but not much more than that. Phillip is trying to take a nap, but I can't imagine him being any more successful at it than he was sleeping last night. He just can't seem to get comfortable." In a lower voice, she added, "I'm considering crushing up a pain pill and lacing his ice cream with it."

"You're letting him have ice cream?" I asked.

"That's what you took away from that? Yes, I'm letting him have whatever he wants, within reason, and no, I would never dose him without his consent." She paused and then added, "At least not yet, anyway."

"I'm sorry. I shouldn't have bothered you," I said as I started to hang up.

"Suzanne, the truth is that I'd love a distraction right now. What's going on?"

"Did you happen to know anything about Jenny White's retreat?"

"Of course I do. She goes every year around this time. Why do you ask?"

"Is there any way we can get in touch with her?" I asked. "Ordinarily I'd never ask, but Mindy Fulbright is using her as an alibi, and I'd really love to know if what she told us was true, that she and Jenny were having dinner when the fire started at ReNEWed."

"Let me see what I can do," Momma said.

"I really don't want to be any trouble," I told her. "You've got enough on your plate as it is."

"Nonsense. If I find anything out, I'll let you know."

"Thanks. Love you," I said.

"Love you right back," she replied.

"Okay, at least for now, Mindy's alibi is up in the air, so she has to stay on our list," I said.

"I agree. Should we go find out what Tyra has to say?"

"I thought we were going to Union Square?" I asked her. "Not that I mind changing up our plans on the fly, but I'm curious."

"The way I see it, we're here, and hopefully, so is Tyra," Grace said with a shrug. "It just makes sense."

Tyra was reluctant to answer the door when we got to her place, and I had to lean on the doorbell for three minutes before she finally answered. When she did, I realized that we'd clearly woken her up. She had a robe wrapped tightly around her, and she was wearing slippers as well. "What's going on, Suzanne? I was sound asleep," she asked as she rubbed her eyes.

I glanced at my watch and saw that it was barely past eight. I'd been getting up so early for so long that I'd forgotten that some people stayed in bed long after I was up and about.

"We're truly sorry about that," I said, doing my best to sound sincere. "Since you're up now though, we wanted to let you know that Gabby woke up yesterday."

"Gabby's awake? That's good news. How's she doing?" she asked as she stifled a yawn.

"Surprisingly well," I answered, and I was very happy that particular statement happened to be true.

"Then maybe she can tell you both that *I* didn't have anything to do with that fire," she said. "Now can I please for the love of all that's pure and good go back to sleep?"

"In a second," Grace said. "The problem is that her memory's still a bit hazy on what led up to the fire, but she should have it all back by this evening. In the meantime, the police are going around getting alibis for everyone who might have been involved. Have they contacted you yet?"

"As a matter of fact, I spoke with the police chief last night," Tyra said, surprising us both. We had been under the impression that Chief Grant wasn't pursuing the case as a criminal investigation. Had something changed his mind after all?

"Really? When was this?" I asked her.

"I ran into him downtown last night," she said. "We discussed the weather, but he never asked me for an alibi. Wouldn't he have taken advantage of the situation while he had me there?"

"This all just came up this morning," I ad-libbed. "I'm sure he'll ask you today. What are you going to tell him?"

It was a bold question, but it was worth a shot.

Her reply was preceded by a heavy sigh, and then she said, "Ladies, as much as I'd love to stand here in my robe and chat with the two of you, I don't have time for this foolishness. I was up past midnight, and I need my sleep."

"What do you make of that?" Grace asked me once we were alone again.

"We clearly woke her up, and she didn't seem particularly upset when we told her that Gabby was awake and that she would soon get her memory back, but maybe Tyra was just too tired to process any of it," I said. "I nearly lost it when she told us that she'd spoken with Stephen last night."

"You recovered nicely," Grace said. "She didn't even bother trying to lie to us by giving us an alibi, did she?"

"No, but I'm not exactly sure we can hold that against her. After all, we did wake her up, and if the roles were reversed, I'm not so sure that I would have reacted any differently than she did, would you have?"

"I guess if I'm being honest, I might not have been as polite as she was," Grace admitted with a wry smile.

"I don't know about you, but I'm starting to feel a little guilty about setting Gabby up like this," I said.

"We agreed that it was the only way to put pressure on our suspects, given the short amount of time we have at our disposal," Grace said.

"I know that, but I still think we need to stop by the hospital and warn her what we're up to. It's on the way to Union Square, and we're going there next anyway. What do you say?"

"It sounds like a plan to me," Grace said.

There was just one problem, though.

When we got to Gabby's room, the chair out front was empty.

It appeared that Bo had left his post, leaving Gabby vulnerable to whoever had attacked her before, and what was worse, we'd just given half our suspects a reason to want to finish the job they'd started earlier.

Chapter 17

My hand shook a little as I reached for the door and pushed it open.

The room was empty, which turned out to be a good thing.

"Are you looking for Gabby?" Penny asked as we nearly ran into her in the hallway. "What a silly question. Of course you are. She's not here anymore."

"She's not back in ICU, is she?" I asked, chilled by the thought that my friend had taken a turn for the worse.

"That's not it at all. One of the VIP suites upstairs opened up, and the big boss had her moved," Penny said with a grin. "Sometimes it pays to have friends in high places."

"Hey, you have connections yourself. After all, you can get free donuts any time you want. That's a perk not *everyone* gets," I told her, relieved that Gabby was all right.

"Believe me, I know it. Oh, I've been told to thank you for the donuts yesterday. They were a big hit around here."

"You are all most welcome," I said. "You know what a fan I am when it comes to nurses and the work they do."

"I do, and on behalf of my brothers and sisters in the field, we thank you," she said with a smile. "Come on, I'll show you where she is now."

As we walked to the elevator, I asked, "Have you met her cousin Bo yet?"

"Oh, Bo and I go way back," Penny said. "In fact, once upon a time, we dated." I couldn't see the beauty and the beast together, and she must have read it in my face. "I had to break up with him, the poor dear."

"Why is that, if you don't mind me asking?" Grace inquired.

"I want to know, too," I added.

"He was just a little *too* sensitive for my taste," Penny admitted.

It was hard to imagine that big and burly man fitting the description. "In what way?"

"A greeting card could make him cry, or even a sweet commercial on television," she said. "I know what he looks like, but deep down, he's really a gentle soul. Did you know he was a poet?"

"As a matter of fact, we did," I said. "Is he any good?"

"He's amazing," she said with a hint of pride in her voice. "He's had work published in some pretty prestigious magazines and journals over the years."

"It sounds as though you're not *completely* over him," I said softly as we rode up to Gabby's floor.

Penny hesitated, and then she admitted, "I *thought* I was, but I've dated some real jerks since we broke up. Maybe I *was* a bit hasty. Do you happen to know if he's seeing anyone?"

"I have no idea, but I'd be more than happy to find out," I said with a grin.

She looked at me for a moment as though she were about to take me up on my offer, but then she shook her head. "No, thanks. I'm sure he's dating someone new by now. I had my chance, and I blew it."

"Penny. Hi!" Bo said enthusiastically as he stood upon our arrival. His face got flushed the moment he saw the nurse, and in his haste, he knocked over the chair he was sitting on as he stood up. "How are you?"

"I'm good, Bo," the nurse said, her face softening on seeing his reaction to her. "How are you?"

"I'm fine. You look amazing," he said softly.

"That's sweet of you to say," she answered, ignoring, or perhaps entirely missing, the obvious care in his voice.

"How's Gabby this morning?" I asked, hating to break up the reunion but not having much choice. We were on a time crunch, and I needed to keep things moving if we were going to be able to solve the case before Gabby lost her protection.

"She's getting a little cranky, which is a good sign, if you ask me. When she was sweet to me yesterday, I almost didn't recognize her," he said with a grin. "You can all go on in."

I hesitated as Penny got a page. "Sorry. They need me back on the floor."

"It was good seeing you," Bo said hopefully.

"You, too," she said as she hurried away.

Bo said softly, more to himself than to us, as she vanished into the elevator, "I miss you."

"She misses you, too, you know," I said.

He looked startled by my comment. "Why do you say that?"

"Ask her out, Bo. I think you'll be pleasantly surprised to hear her answer," I said.

He looked a little dejected at the suggestion. "I don't think so. She was pretty clear about where things stood when she broke up with me the last time."

"Hey, it's still worth a shot, isn't it?" Grace asked him.

"Maybe," he said. "Anyway, you two should go on in."

I looked at Grace with one raised eyebrow. Usually *I* was the one who meddled in other people's love lives. She just shrugged, ending the conversation. It was that way with us sometimes.

There was no need for words between us, and a few looks were all that we required to communicate volumes.

"What have you two been up to? Have you been able to find out who tried to get rid of me? And knowing why would be nice, too. Come on. Let's hear it. I don't have all day," the patient demanded.

It appeared that Bo had been right.

If Gabby's current attitude and demeanor were any indication of her general state of being, she was definitely getting better.

"Listen, you're probably not going to like this, but we didn't see any other way to make things happen," I said after taking a deep breath.

"And you didn't think to get my approval first?" she asked. "That's so typical of you, Suzanne. What possessed you to do something you *knew* that I wouldn't approve of?"

I thought the criticism was patently unfair, and I was about to say so when Grace surprised us both by speaking up. "Gabby, you don't even know what we did yet. Shouldn't you wait to at least hear us out before you start slinging around blame?"

Gabby looked shocked for a moment, and then, to my surprise as well as Grace's, she backpedaled immediately. "I'm sorry. You're right."

"Excuse me? What did you just say?" Grace asked her, clearly unsure as to what she'd just heard.

Gabby grinned for a split second, and I knew that we were going to be all right. "You heard me the first time, so don't expect me to repeat it." She then turned to me and asked, "What exactly did you do that you need to ask forgiveness for instead of permission?"

"We used you as bait," I said as plainly and simply as I could.

"Go on. I'm listening," Gabby said with a look of concentration. "Tell me more."

"We implied that you will, without a doubt, get your complete memory back by the end of the day, and that at that time you'll know whoever it was that attacked you in your shop and then burned Re-NEWed to the ground," I replied. "Given the deadline of how short a period of time Bo can stay here watching over you, we thought it was the only way to make things happen fast."

"I think it's a marvelous idea," Gabby said with a grin. "I'm proud of you both for coming up with it."

"Does that mean that you're okay with us painting a target on your back?" Grace asked her, clearly surprised yet again by Gabby's reaction.

"It should get results, and that's all that really counts," Gabby said enthusiastically. "I feel as though I've been sitting around waiting for the other shoe to drop since I woke up. I can't go around for the rest of my life looking over my shoulder, wondering when the arsonist is going to attack again. This way we can flush out whoever did it, and we're done with it once and for all."

I knew from experience that it wasn't going to be nearly as easy as that, but I wasn't about to point that out to Gabby. We could be in for some perilous times in the course of the next twenty-four hours, and I was afraid that she wasn't taking it seriously enough. "We're assuming a great many things here, Gabby," I explained, "not the least of which is that Bo can handle anyone who comes after you."

"Don't you worry about Bo," Gabby said. "He may have the heart of a poet, but he's got the build and general disposition of a middle linebacker. He and his friends can more than handle the worm who hit me from behind. So, who have you told so far, and how did they react?"

"We've spoken with Tyra and Mindy," I said, "with mixed results. Tyra wouldn't give us an alibi, and when we pushed her on it, she left us standing there on her doorstep and went back to bed."

Gabby shrugged. "She's been a night owl her entire life, so I'm not really surprised you woke her up banging on her door this early in the morning. What did Mindy say?"

"She gave us something, but actually, it was a pretty weak alibi," I said, not wanting to go into details about Mindy's aborted date with their common boyfriend if I could help it. "Momma's helping us check up on it, but in the meantime, Mindy has to stay on our list."

"Good, you've got the whole crew working on it," Gabby said, clearly glad that we'd called in reinforcements. "What about Jake? What's he doing?"

"At the moment, Jake is working with the Union Square police to help solve a rash of robberies they've been having lately," I said. "But he's there to advise us if we need it."

"I heard about that masked robber," Gabby said. "I'm glad your husband is pitching in. It's a sad thing when a small business owner has to worry about getting robbed by someone other than their suppliers and customers. So, what's next on your list?"

"We're heading to Union Square to have a chat with Manny and Buster," Grace said.

"Gabby, there's something I've been wanting to ask you. Who do *you* think hit you and set your shop on fire?" I asked her. It was a delicate question to ask, but I really wanted to know what she thought about it.

She shrugged again. "If I had to guess, I'd say that it could be any one of them," Gabby replied. "I keep having this feeling that I can see who attacked me, but the harder I focus on it, the faster it vanishes. It's so frustrating losing part of my memory."

"Don't fight it," Grace said. "It will come back when you least expect it."

"I hope you're right. Evidently there's a chance that I'll *never* get the last day before the attack back." She looked desolate about the prospect, and I knew there was nothing I could do about that, so I decided to change the subject.

"Gabby, do me a favor and rate our suspects as to how likely they are to have done it, if you can." I pushed a little harder. "Come on, I know you've been thinking about this since you woke up. How could you not?"

She looked a little troubled by the question. "It's true enough. I've had time to think about little else," she admitted. "If I had to have a favorite, I'd pick Buster. The long shot would be Mindy, and I'd say that Manny and Tyra are somewhere in between."

"Do you really think Buster did it?" Grace asked him.

"It sounds like something he would do," she said. "Suzanne, if he *was* responsible for burning my place to the ground, Donut Hearts has got to be next on his list."

"That's why we're trying to catch whoever did it before they can strike again," I said as calmly as I could. I couldn't stand the thought of *my* shop being attacked. There was so much of my heart and soul in the place that I wasn't sure that I'd ever be able to recover. "Gabby, how are you doing?"

She tried to blow off my question and my obvious concern. "I've got a headache you wouldn't believe, and it's still kind of hard to breathe, but other than those two things, I'm just dandy."

I wasn't going to let her get away with being so dismissive. I reached out and took her hand in mine, and then I asked her again. "I'm talking about ReNEWed being gone, and you know it."

Gabby started to tear up, but somehow, as though by sheer willpower alone, she stopped the sudden display of emotion. "The truth of the matter is that I'm trying not to think about it at the moment," she admitted. "Otherwise it would be too painful to deal with. Thanks for asking, though."

"Once this is over, if there's anything I can do, and I mean anything, to help you get back on your feet, all you have to do is ask."

"That offer includes me, too," Grace said as she reached out and took Gabby's other hand.

"I appreciate that." She choked out the words, and then, while she could still trust herself to speak, she added, "Now get out of here and go find the lunatic that tried to burn me up along with my shop."

We hesitated at Bo's station once we were outside of Gabby's room.

"How's she doing?" Bo asked us anxiously.

"She's more fragile than I've ever seen her," I admitted, "but the woman's got fire and spunk, and if anybody can bounce back from this, it's her. Keep an eye on her, Bo."

"I will," he said.

"Have you thought any more about asking Penny out again?" Grace asked him with a slight smile.

"I'm still pondering," Bo answered.

"Well, don't ponder too long," I answered. "You don't want to let a chance for happiness slip through your fingers. Life is short."

"I know it only too well," he said. "I won't take forever, but I'm just not ready yet to put myself out there again."

"Just don't wait too long," I told him.

Chapter 18

We were on our way to Union Square when my cell phone rang. "It's Momma," I said as I answered it and put the call on speaker. "Hey, Momma. How's Phillip doing?" It was my go-to reaction since his surgery, and I was starting to understand why he didn't want anyone to know what he'd gone through. He didn't want his cancer to define him, or his mortality. Jake had implied as much earlier, but I hadn't seen it until that moment in my own reaction.

"He's doing a bit better," she said, "but that's not why I'm calling. I just spoke with Jenny."

"How did you manage that? I thought the ban on outside communication was unbreakable," I answered. My mother was something to reckon with, but even *she* had her limits, which was hard for me to realize sometimes.

"She wasn't at the retreat yet," Momma said. "I got her on her cell phone as she was on her way. She confirmed Mindy's story. They were together for an hour and a half, from a quarter till six until a quarter after seven. That's more than the time you needed to be sure of, wasn't it? Clearly Mindy didn't do it."

"Was she positive about the exact time?" I asked Momma.

"Oh, she knew it well. It seems that Mindy spent the entire meal they were together lamenting over her lost love. Jenny said she kept checking her watch the whole time she was over there, so she knew *ex-*

actly how long she was there. There's no denying the fact that Mindy Fulbright is in the clear."

"Thanks, Momma. You're the best," I said.

"This was one of the easiest things you could ask me to do," Momma said. "Next time, give me something more difficult, will you?"

"I'll try," I answered with a grin as I hung up.

Grace hadn't said a word, but once the phone call had ended, she said, "So that takes Mindy off our list once and for all."

"I'd say that's progress," I said.

"We still have three likely suspects though, and remember, Gabby herself said that Mindy was a long shot," Grace reminded me.

"I didn't say we were ready to accuse the arsonist yet, but when it comes to potential bad guys, you have to agree that three is better than four."

"And one is even better," Grace said. "Suzanne, we've got to make something happen while Gabby is still under Bo's protection."

"I agree that time is of the essence, but do you honestly think Bo is going to abandon his post just because the hospital administrator says he has to leave?"

"No, but Gabby can't keep looking over her shoulder for the rest of her life, either," Grace said.

"We'll make something happen," I said with more confidence than I felt. I'd never put myself under such a strict deadline before, and I didn't like it. My style was not nearly so aggressive usually, but special times called for special measures. At least I had Grace with me. Between the two of us, we'd make something happen if it were at all possible.

After all, Gabby was counting on us.

"I don't have any more time for the two of you," Manny said the moment we walked through the door of his store. The place had just opened a few minutes earlier, and at least for the moment, we had the owner to ourselves. "We've got a busy day ahead of us."

"Then we'll make it quick," I said. "I thought you might like an update. Is Buster around?"

"He's in back," Manny said, "but he's busy. Whatever you've got to say, you can say it to me, and I'll tell him later."

That wouldn't do at all, since I wanted to gauge both men's reactions to the news that Gabby's memory was coming back, and I couldn't do that if I wasn't the one who broke the news. "Get him, Manny. It won't take long."

He looked at me stubbornly, clearly about to refuse again, when Grace piped up, "We'd be glad to hang around if it's not convenient now. I'm sure Buster will be out here sometime today, and while we're waiting, we can talk in front of your customers about everything we know about who might have tried to kill our friend, including the two of you."

Manny stared at her for a long second, and then he called out, "Buster, get out here." While we were waiting, he snapped, "Make it quick."

"We will," I promised.

As Buster walked out, he asked, "What's up, boss?" And then he spotted us. "Hey," he said uncertainly.

"Hey," I answered brightly. "We've got good news. Gabby's memory is coming back. The doctors say that by this evening, she'll remember everything that happened the day of the fire."

"That's good news," Manny said, clearly distracted by something.

"Yeah, I'm glad, too," Buster added, not sounding nearly so convincing.

"Have you told Tyra yet?" Manny asked us.

"Yes," I said, but I was confused by his question. "Manny, are you dating her, too?"

"You didn't know that?" Manny asked, looking angry with himself for inadvertently helping us. "We went out a few times, right up until the day before the fire. She didn't make the cut, so I dumped her. I figured Gabby had already blabbed to you about Tyra. She found out by accident, but it was no big deal."

"I'm not sure Tyra felt that way," I said.

"Listen, I know you both think I'm a bad man, and maybe I'm not the greatest guy in the world, but I'm happy Gabby's getting her memory back," Buster interjected. "If it really happens, she'll be the first one to tell you that I didn't do it, but I have my doubts."

"The doctors seemed pretty certain that it would," I said, trying to see why Buster sounded so confident.

"Yeah, well, if they said that, they're lying to you. I looked it up on the Internet. In a lot of cases like this, those memories *never* come back," he said matter-of-factly.

Maybe *that* was why he was so assured in his statement. Buster believed we were bluffing, and he was going all in on his bet.

A few customers poked their heads in the door. "Are you open yet?"

Manny put on his best smile. "Come on in and have a look around." He then turned to us and said in a near whisper, "You've said what you needed to say, and now you two have to go."

It was clear we'd gotten all we were going to get out of both men, so I turned to Grace and said, "He's right. Let's head out."

Grace nodded, and once we were outside, she asked, "Can you believe Manny was seeing Tyra, too?"

"The fact that he dumped her just before the fire looks bad, too," I said. "Do you think it's odd that Tyra didn't say a word about going out with Manny to us?"

"It's not something you'd want to voluntarily bring up though, is it? Remember what Mindy confessed to after we pressed her on it? She *knew* what Manny was capable of, and yet she still asked him over for dinner," Grace said as we headed back to my Jeep.

"That's true, but we still need to ask Tyra about it, and press her even harder for an alibi," I said. "Are you up for another drive back to April Springs?"

"You could probably make that trip with your eyes closed," Grace said as I started off.

"Maybe, but if it's all the same to you, I'm not going to try it," I said with a grin.

We were getting closer.

I could feel it in my bones.

Something told me that there was just one more missing piece, and then everything would come together once we had it.

The problem now was knowing where to look for it.

Chapter 19

"We need to face facts, Suzanne. Tyra's not here," Grace said after we spent six minutes knocking on Tyra's door, ringing the bell, and even walking around the house, searching for some sign that the woman was ducking us.

"Or she's not answering the bell this time," I replied. I started pounding again, long past trying to be subtle about my demand to see her. I wasn't sure how she'd react if she ever did come to the door, but apparently we weren't going to find out.

"She could be gone," Grace said.

"Do you think she ran away?" I asked. "It's going to make her look guilty if she just took off."

"Suzanne, I didn't mean that she's gone for good. What if she's off shopping, or out having an early lunch? We can't just assume that she ran."

"But what if she did? We need to call Chief Grant and at least let him know what's going on," I insisted.

Grace stepped between me and the door I was currently assaulting. "And tell him what, exactly? That we think someone he isn't searching for is missing in a case he doesn't believe exists? You know him well enough to guess how he'd react to that particular phone call."

I nodded. "You're right."

"Besides, he's not all that thrilled that we're stirring things up when there's no direct evidence to...wait. What did you just say?" She looked clearly puzzled by my response. "Did you just admit that I was right?"

"I did. Grace, we can only do so much. We have no official status even when the police believe that a crime has been committed. I know I'm grasping at straws. I'm just really worried about Gabby."

"Have a little faith. We'll figure this out, Suzanne," Grace said. "Just because we're out of leads doesn't mean that we have to give up."

"What else is there for us to do?" I asked her. "I mean it. Manny and Buster are both stonewalling us, and we can't find Tyra. We can't exactly look over what we believe is a crime scene, since it's ash and rubble at the moment. Gabby hasn't regained her memory of what happened, or we would have heard from her. I don't know what else we *can* do." I felt as defeated as I had in a long time, and I didn't like the feeling. I had enjoyed a particularly long run of good luck in solving the cases I chose to investigate on my own, with help from a variety of the people closest to me, including Grace, Jake, Momma, Phillip, and even George, but it appeared that streak was about to come to an end unless Gabby got her memory back or we managed to come up with a new clue.

I was beginning to believe that neither one of those things was going to happen.

"I've got an idea," Grace said.

"I'm certainly open to suggestions," I admitted. "Anything you can come up with has to be better than just standing around waiting for the other shoe to drop."

"Let's go have lunch," Grace said.

"How exactly is that going to help further our investigation?" I asked her.

"I doubt that it will, but it seems to me this is as good a time as any to regroup. I truly believe that we'll come up with something."

"And if we don't?" I asked her.

"At least we'll get to eat," Grace answered with a grin.

I couldn't deny her logic. "Okay. I'm sold. Besides, we promised Trish that we'd have lunch with her, so at least we can keep our word to *one* of our friends."

Grace touched my shoulder lightly. "Suzanne, we haven't given up on helping Gabby, but we're certainly entitled to stop and eat a meal every now and then."

"Okay," I said smiling slightly. "You're right. Let me just do one thing first."

"What's possibly more important than eating?" she asked me, returning my grin with one of her own.

"I want to leave Tyra a note to call me, just in case she isn't gone for good." I scrawled out a quick message and jammed it in the gap between the door and the casing. If she came in that way, she'd either see the note or it would flutter to the ground, and that would have to catch her attention. Whether she'd do as I'd asked and call me was another thing altogether, but it was the best thing I could think of, so I did it.

Once that was accomplished, I turned to Grace and said, "Come on. You did such a good job cheering me up that I'm buying today."

"I appreciate the offer, but we don't do that anymore, remember?" she answered with a grin of her own.

"You're right," I answered. "I hope that it's the thought that counts, then."

"It is," she replied as we walked back to my Jeep and headed toward our favorite place to eat in all of April Springs, which, given the real lack of competition, wasn't saying much, but it still counted for something. Not only was Trish's food delicious, but it was always a pleasure seeing her friendly face, and at the moment, we could use all of those we could get.

The Boxcar Grill was so busy that it appeared there wasn't a chance Trish was going to be able to eat with us after all. "Hey, Trish. If it's all the same to you, we'll take a rain check for that lunch," I told her as we muscled our way through the crowd of folks waiting for a table.

"There is no way I'm letting you two off the hook that easily," Trish said as she pointed to the table closest to the door. It had a Reserved sign on it, and a great many people were staring at it, wondering what sort of local celebrity merited a reservation at a place that didn't allow them.

"We don't mind coming back at a better time, at the very least," I said. "Seriously, it's not worth aggravating any of your customers for us."

Trish frowned. "We had plans, though."

"Plans change," I told her. "We're not all that hungry anyway," I lied. "That was a massive breakfast."

"Okay, if you're sure," Trish said. It was clear that she was at least a little relieved that I'd insisted we postpone the get-together. She'd tried to get a new employee to help out up front at the register before, but it had always turned into a debacle, and she was soon back at her usual station. I knew how lucky I was to have Emma and Sharon available and eager to step into my shoes on a moment's notice at the donut shop, and while I couldn't afford to reward their loyalty monetarily all of the time, I always made sure they knew how much I appreciated both of them, and at least so far, that seemed to be enough.

"I expect you both back here later," Trish said as she pulled the sign off the table. Four people clearly not together happily scooped up the suddenly free seats.

"We'll see you soon," I said with a smile as Grace and I exited.

"That was a nice thing to do and all, but the truth of the matter is that I'm still hungry," Grace said with a frown.

"We could always drop by the donut shop and grab something there," I offered.

"Okay. At the very least I can get something to hold me until we can eat a proper meal." She quickly added, "Not that your donuts aren't proper and all."

"Easy, girl, I'm not about to suggest that donuts are a substitute for a balanced meal. I sell treats, goodies that are to be savored, but I have no delusions that anyone should eat them as a regular meal. Well, maybe breakfast, but lunch? Why do you think I close the shop at eleven every day?"

"Because you haven't been able to convince people that donuts at noon are a good thing, or because you're there at three a.m. every morning and you're tired of working by then, so you close up so you can go home, take a shower, and then catch a nap?"

"I'd say both scenarios pretty much sum up the situation," I said with a smile. "Come on. You have to at least let me buy you a donut."

"Considering they don't cost you anything, at least any cash, I might even take two."

There was a problem, though.

Even though it was four minutes before eleven, not yet our standard closing time, the shop was empty, the door was locked, and there was no sign of Emma and Sharon inside.

Maybe I'd been a little too hasty with my praise for them after all.

"Hey, Emma. How's it going?" I asked when she picked up my call. I was about to ask her why Donut Hearts was closed when she interrupted me before I could follow up.

"Suzanne, you're never going to believe what happened today. It was the wildest thing. A tour bus got lost, and everyone on it was starving. Evidently the driver was new, and he missed a turn or something and was too proud to ask for directions. Anyway, a little after ten, the door opened and around thirty starving seniors piled in. They bought us out! What they didn't eat in the shop they took to go. We made some serious coin today, my friend."

"So there was no reason to stay open," I said.

"I suppose we could have kept the place going and served coffee, but that would have probably just frustrated everyone that they couldn't get any treats. It's great news, isn't it?"

"It certainly is, but maybe if that ever happens again, you could leave a sign on the front door explaining the situation so folks will know why we're not open." It was a gentle suggestion, but I really didn't want to aggravate our regulars who might come by expecting donuts only to be greeted by a darkened shop.

"Did I forget to do that?" she asked, sounding upset. "Mom told me to do it, but I guess I just forgot. I'm so sorry. I guess I was so excited that it completely slipped my mind. Suzanne, I'm really sorry."

"No harm, no foul, Emma," I said. "I'll see you tomorrow."

"You're coming in?" she asked, clearly unhappy with my response. "Are you taking away our two days of running the shop just because of one simple mistake? Mom's going to kill me."

"Take it easy, Emma. I just forgot that I was off tomorrow, too. I'm not punishing you."

"Thanks. She's saving up for another trip to Ireland, and she'd be furious if she lost the job as my assistant at Donut Hearts on your days off."

"There are no worries on that front. We're good," I said. After I hung up, I turned to Grace. "Well, it appears that you and I were destined not to eat lunch today."

"We can't give up yet," Grace said. "Surely there's *someplace* open around here where we can get something to eat."

"We could always make something ourselves," I suggested.

Grace frowned. "I don't know about you, but my fridge doesn't have enough in it to feed *me*, let alone both of us."

"I have a lasagna in the fridge from two nights ago," I admitted. "I know it's not Napoli's quality, and it's a leftover to boot, but if you'd like some, you're more than welcome to it."

"Sold," Grace said. "I'll take your leftovers over my fresh meals any day of the week."

"I've even got some salad greens left, too. We'll have ourselves a little feast and try to forget that we're failing at finding the arsonist who started the fire at ReNEWed."

"Suzanne, we're not giving up, remember?"

"That's right, we're regrouping, whatever that means," I said as we walked back to my Jeep, still sitting in the Boxcar Grill's nearly full parking lot. Driving home was a breeze since it was so close, and I didn't like the idea of my Jeep being in that jammed lot unattended. In the course of things, it was still relatively new, at least in my mind, and I hated every added ding and dent I got from other parked cars.

I was reheating the lasagna while Grace set the table when my cell phone rang. Maybe it was from Gabby, or even Tyra, but when I saw it was my husband, I was just as happy about it.

Talking to Jake was always a good thing, even when the news wasn't.

"Sorry, I can't talk," Jake said the moment I answered.

"Hey, you called me, remember?" I asked him, but I was talking to dead air.

"What was that all about?" Grace asked me.

"I honestly have no idea," I said.

"Aren't you going to call him back?"

"No, he's obviously into something that needs his full attention, and I'm not about to distract him from that, whatever it might be."

Grace laughed. "You two are the perfect pair, aren't you?"

"I'd like to think so," I said. "Why do you say that, though?"

"You both love digging into problems and looking for answers almost as much as you love each other," she replied.

"That's certainly true enough," I said. "I never really thought about it that way before."

"That's because you're too close to it to see how things really are between you."

"Speaking of relationships, how are things going between you and our police chief?"

Grace grinned. "As a matter of fact, they are so good that I'm afraid I'll jinx things by talking about them. Isn't that lasagna ready yet?"

I'd been microwaving it on half power, and it took a while, but I'd found that reheating it slowly gave it a much better taste and consistency than blasting it on full. Doing it in the oven would have been better still, but Grace and I didn't have that much time on our hands, even if we were temporarily stymied by the case we were working on.

We had just sat down to eat when my phone rang again.

"It's probably just Jake again. I'll call him back later," I said, trying to ignore the summons.

"Take the call, Suzanne. I know you love me, so I'm not offended that I'll always be second in your heart."

"Does that count Momma, too?" I asked her with a grin as I reached for my phone.

"Okay, third then, but if I'm any lower than that, please don't tell me," she said.

"You'll always be third to me," I said with a grin as I answered.

It wasn't Jake, though.

The moment I heard Bo's voice, I knew that something had happened, and most likely, it was something bad.

Chapter 20

"Suzanne, we had an incident here a few minutes ago, and I knew you'd want to hear about it," Bo said.

"Is Gabby okay?" I asked, suddenly realizing how much I'd risked by putting her in jeopardy, even if she had approved it after the fact.

"Relax, Suzanne. She's fine. Manny Wright just left here, and he wasn't very happy about being turned away, I can tell you that."

"What happened?" I asked as I put the phone on speaker.

"He tried to force his way past me and get into her room," Bo said with a hint of laughter in his voice. "Can you imagine that? I told him to stop, and when he wouldn't listen, I had to persuade him that his current course of action wasn't going to work out too well for him."

"Did he say *why* he wanted to see your cousin?" Grace asked. "Hi, Bo, it's me."

"Hey, Grace. Yeah, if you can believe it, he kept saying that she was the one he loved, that he'd made a huge mistake with the other women, and that he needed to see her. He said that almost losing her was more than he could take, and it made him realize just what he'd thrown away."

That certainly sounded like a different story than we'd ever heard from him. "Did you believe him?" I asked.

"No, not a chance. He clearly had an ulterior motive, but I wasn't about to risk finding out what it was. I sent him packing, and then I told Gabby what happened."

"What did she say?"

"That I did the right thing," Bo admitted. "It was nice hearing that from her. Anyway, I just thought you should know."

"Thanks for calling, Bo. Keep us posted, okay?"

"Will do," he said, and then he quickly added, "Here comes Penny. Gotta go."

"Ask her out, you big dweeb," Grace shouted, but it was too late. He'd already hung up.

I looked at Grace and smiled. "Dweeb? Really?"

"It was the only thing I could come up with on the spur of the moment. Do you believe Manny's story?"

"I'm with Bo. We haven't seen *anything* from Manny to make me think that he cares about Gabby one way or the other. There has to be another reason he was so determined to see her."

"I'm not completely convinced myself," Grace said.

"What do you mean?"

"What if he was telling the truth? I know, I'm supposed to be the hardhearted one, but it's possible, isn't it? If Manny wanted to hurt Gabby, he wouldn't have tried to push his way past Bo. Not only would that make him a witness that Manny was even there, but I don't know about you, but I wouldn't want Bo angry or upset with me."

"No, I wouldn't, either," I said. After giving it a moment's thought, I said, "I can see another reason it might have played out that way. Let's say Manny came to the hospital to finish the job, thinking he could slip in and out without being seen. Maybe he saw Bo too late, so he was committed to doing *something*, and knowing Manny, using love as a cover sounds exactly like something he would do. He forced the issue by claiming his love for Gabby to hide the fact that he was really there to hurt her. It's at least possible, isn't it?"

Grace nodded. "I hate to admit it, but I think you're right. I must be getting soft."

"I'd *never* say that about you," I said as I patted her hand. "That was supposed to be a compliment, in case you weren't sure. Grace, your pragmatism is part of your charm."

"Thanks. I guess being in love has affected my way of looking at the world lately," she admitted. Before taking a bite of lasagna, she quickly added, "And that's all that we need to talk about that."

"Got it," I said as I took a bite myself. It was really rather good, though not as tasty as it had been fresh out of the oven. Then again, it was there, it was free, and I was hungry, so everything worked out for the best in the end after all, at least as far as lunch was concerned.

As we were cleaning up, I got the call I'd been expecting earlier.

It was Jake again.

"Can you talk this time? What was that all about earlier?" I asked him.

"Suzanne, I have some news you're going to want to hear."

"Fire away," I answered as I put my phone on speaker so Grace could hear, too.

"Buster Breckinridge is on the run."

Chapter 21

"What do you mean, he's on the run?" I asked. "Does that mean that *he's* the one who burned Gabby's shop down after all?"

"No, in fact, he's got a pretty good alibi for the time of the fire," Jake said.

"I can't wait to hear what it is," Grace said.

"The thing is, he couldn't have set the fire at ReNEWed, because at the time, he was leaving Peggy's Pet Supplies in Union Square after robbing the place."

"How could you possibly know that?" I asked him.

"I've been going around to businesses near where the robberies occurred, looking at video surveillance files, and on the fourth try, I found a clear shot of Buster taking off the dog's head mask Peggy reported the robber was wearing ninety seconds *after* the robbery. By the time I got to the Garden Center, he had already taken off. Evidently Manny left him in charge while he went to run an errand, and Buster cleaned out the register before he took off. Manny's ready to kill him."

"That was some good police work, Jake," I said.

"It was okay, but I should have been able to arrest him and hand him over to Chief Erskine in a neat little package," Jake said, the disappointment clear in his voice.

"Could you have done that legally without making a citizen's arrest?" Grace asked him.

"Actually, the chief gave me temporary status to make arrests this morning," Jake admitted, and then he quickly added, "Suzanne, I wasn't taking any chances. I had the chief meet me at the Garden Center. I just happened to get there thirty seconds before Manny showed up. That's when he discovered that he'd been robbed too, and the chief came not a minute later. I never really did anything risky."

That wasn't strictly true—he'd taken a chance going to brace a convicted felon alone—but I wasn't about to chastise him for it. After all, he'd deserved to make the arrest after doing the required police work in order to find him. "What did the chief say?" I asked.

"He was upset with himself for not checking the security footage around the robberies himself," Jake told us, "but he's young, and he's got good instincts. Anyway, I'll be home in a few hours. I'm going to help out with the manhunt, if you're okay with me doing it."

"I'm fine with it, Jake. Be careful," I said as I started to hang up.

"You, too," he said, and then the call was over.

"You're really okay with him going after Buster?" Grace asked me.

"I'm fine with it," I said. "Jake needs this, and I'm not about to take it away from him. Hey, he just made our job easier. I get why Buster didn't want to give us his real alibi. It would be tough to admit that he couldn't have burned down Gabby's shop and assaulted her because he was busy robbing another shop half an hour away at the exact same time. No wonder he was happy Gabby's memory might have been coming back, as unconvincing as he was telling us."

"And then there were two," Grace said. "It looks as though Manny is in the lead, doesn't it?"

"True, but I still think Tyra is a likely suspect. All we have to do now is find her."

"Suzanne, I said it before, and I'll say it again. There's a good chance that she hasn't gone anywhere farther from home than the grocery store. Why don't we finish cleaning up here and then go by her place again to see if she's there, by any chance? What do you say?"

"I'd say it's about the *only* thing we can do right now," I answered. "Poor Gabby. I'd hate to have so many suspects involved if something ever happened to me."

"I wouldn't care how many people wanted to see you dead," Grace said. "I'd track whoever did it down and make them pay for what they did to you, even if it took the rest of my life."

"I'd do the same thing for you," I admitted. "It's what being friends is all about, isn't it?"

"For the two of us, at any rate. Come on. Let's go see if we can find Tyra Hitchings and get her to at least give us an alibi."

There was no answer at Tyra's, but I noticed something the moment we walked up the steps.

The note I'd left there for her earlier was now gone.

"At least we know that she's been here, Grace," I said, pointing to the spot I'd left my request for her to call me.

"Maybe," Grace answered. "What if someone else took it?"

"Why would anyone do that?"

"What if they didn't want Tyra talking to us?" she asked. "We know for a fact that Manny was in town earlier. Maybe he saw it and grabbed it before she could get it."

Something suddenly occurred to me that I hadn't even considered before. "Grace, I just had a crazy thought."

"Don't keep it to yourself. What is it?" Grace asked as she moved away from the front door and headed back to the Jeep.

As I followed her, I asked her, "Do you think it's possible that we're looking for *two* people and not *one*?"

"Do you honestly think that it's possible that Manny and Tyra conspired to hit Gabby over the head and then burn her shop down? I honestly can't see the two of them working together on *anything*."

"I can't, either," I said. "But what if the person who hit Gabby wasn't the same one who started the fire?"

She mulled it over as we got into my Jeep. "It's possible, I suppose," she allowed.

"Let's go to Union Square and ask Manny," I said. "At least we've got a pretty good chance of finding him at his shop."

As we made our way out of town and drove past the hospital, I asked, "I wonder if Gabby's had any luck getting her memory back? Should we stop in and see how she's doing?"

"Maybe we should go find Manny first," Grace said. "After all, I'm sure that Bo or Penny will call us the second anything changes with Gabby's status."

"You're right," I said. "I wonder if those two will give it another go?"

"We've both certainly done all that *we* can to push them together," Grace said. "Suzanne, you're a bad influence on me. You know that, don't you?"

"What did I do?" I asked her. "You were all for meddling in their lives all by yourself."

"I know, but I've seen you do it so many times that I couldn't seem to help myself," she answered with a slight smile.

I shrugged. "What can I say? I've discovered that when you're in love, you want the whole world to be in love, too."

After a few more minutes of driving, Grace said, "Wow, Jake wrapped that case up pretty quickly, didn't he?"

"I don't think it's Chief Erskine's fault that he didn't think to look at other video security footages from around the crime scenes," I said. "Jake has an awful lot of experience in this."

"It's almost as though he were born to it," Grace said softly.

"You don't have to tiptoe around it with me," I answered. "I know that Jake's got to get back into law enforcement in at least some capacity, even if it's just working as a consultant. We discussed it last night, but I'm not sure if he's really ready to commit to doing it, no matter what he says. I want to discuss it with him more, but I'm just not sure how I'm going to bring it up with him. He told me that he wanted to wait and see how this case turned out, but he solved it so quickly I don't see how he can just turn his back on what he's clearly so very good at."

"You're not going to suggest that he go back to the state police, are you?" she asked me. "It's going to take him away from you for long stretches of time."

"Trust me, I know that better than anyone else, but he's got to find some meaning in his life, some purpose besides just being with me, no matter what it ends up being. Don't worry. We'll make things work, no matter what."

She reached over and patted my shoulder gently. "I know you will. If there's anything in the world I have faith in, it's the two of you."

"Hey, is that Tyra?" I asked Grace as we neared Manny's shop. I was about to pull into the garden center's parking lot when she passed us on foot going quickly in the other direction, so I kept driving until I could turn around and go back to talk to her. "Has she been crying? She looks miserable."

That's when Grace shouted, "Look! Manny's following her. Suzanne, what's going on?"

"I have no idea, but we're about to find out," I said as I whipped around and did a U-turn.

Grace asked, "What are you going to do?"

"My Jeep is too recognizable," I said. "I'm going to park somewhere so Manny won't see it if he heads back this way. I want to catch him off guard, and if he sees my vehicle, he'll have time to prepare for us."

"Okay, but find someplace fast," she said, and then she grabbed my arm, the one I was steering with at the moment, almost sending me into the other lane of oncoming traffic. I whipped the Jeep into a nearby parking spot on the street and tried to get my nerves back under control.

"Grace, don't do that!"

"I'm sorry, but I had to get your attention. Suzanne, they're coming back this way! Is he actually chasing her down the street toward us?"

"Duck down," I ordered. There wasn't a lot of room in the front of the Jeep to hide in, but we managed to slump down in our seats enough for them to miss seeing us as they hurried past. I wasn't sure we needed to bother. They were both so focused on each other that I doubted either one of them would have spotted us if we had been waving flags and shouting their names.

Once they were past us, I started to get out when Grace asked, "What are you doing now?"

"I want to get close enough to hear what they're saying," I said.

We were out on the sidewalk and heading after them in moments. Tyra was fast, quicker than I would have expected, and Manny was lagging behind a bit. He was still in hot pursuit, if you could call it that, but Tyra was clearly outdistancing him. We were back to his shop's parking lot when I saw Tyra jump into her car and drive off. Manny got into a black SUV, and he was on her tail before we had time to turn around and head back to my Jeep.

Grace and I were the ones running now.

By the time we got back to my car and started the engine, it appeared that we'd lost them.

I wasn't going to just give up, though.

I had a feeling that we had just witnessed a confrontation between a would-be killer and their accuser.

The only problem was that we still didn't know which was which.

Chapter 22

"Where did they go?" I asked as I frantically drove on in the direction we'd last seen the two vehicles speeding away from us. "How could we lose them so quickly? They were in sight just a few seconds ago."

"Maybe so, but they were both flying when we saw them," she said. "They could be anywhere by now."

As we raced out of town, the woods grew around us quickly on either side. Union Square had stopped developing in this direction, probably because there was such a steep drop-off on either side of the road. The woods here were dense, and it must have been difficult to build on.

I was driving faster than I should have been when Grace grabbed my arm again.

"Would you please stop doing that?" I asked her fiercely.

"I'm sorry, but I think I just saw something back there," she said. "Turn around. Better yet, pull off the road."

"Where exactly am I supposed to do that?" I asked. There was no room at all on either side of the road.

"I don't care, but we need to get back there. Suzanne, I think Manny and Tyra just had an accident."

I found a spot a few hundred yards up the road, pulled the Jeep into it, and we hurried back on foot to where Grace had seen something moments before.

"Should I call the police?" Grace asked me as she pulled out her cell phone.

"No, let's see what's going on first," I said.

We made our way to the spot in question, and as I looked down into a small ravine, I could see something shiny amidst the greenery. How anything managed to catch the light in such a densely wooded area was beyond me. "There's *something* down there," I said as I picked my way quickly down the steep slope. "How did you see anything from the road, going as fast as we were going?"

"The branches were broken and bent along here," she said. "I knew something was wrong."

"It's Manny's SUV," I said as we got closer and I recognized the first vehicle.

"That's not all," Grace said as she pointed ahead of it. "That's Tyra's car in front of it."

"He must have pushed her off the road, and then he ended up going in after her," I said. It was the only scenario that made sense. There wasn't much of a turn where they'd gone over the edge, and it was a beautiful day without a drop of rain in sight.

It had to be deliberate!

I held my breath for a second as I approached Manny's vehicle, bracing myself for what I was probably going to find inside.

To my surprise though, it was empty!

While I'd gone straight to Manny's car, Grace had made her way over to Tyra's. "She's not here!" Grace called out.

"Neither is Manny, but there's blood on the seat *and* the door handle," I said. Both air bags had gone off, probably saving their lives.

But they'd still been in an accident, and both of them had evidently managed to walk away from it.

The only real question at the moment was, where had they gone?

Chapter 23

I pulled out my phone to call it in, but I couldn't get a signal. We were below grade and in the thick of a dense canopy of trees, so it was no wonder I couldn't get through.

"I can't get a signal," I said as I put my phone away. "You were right. We should have called it in before."

"Should we climb back up and call 911?" Grace asked.

"No, there's no time," I said. I chewed the situation over in my mind, and then I added, "On second thought, if you want to call, you can climb back up by yourself, but I'm going to go see what's going on. I don't want to risk being too late to save Tyra."

"I'm going with you," she said resolutely. "No matter what happens, we're going to be together."

"Then let's go."

We made our way deeper and deeper into the woods.

It wasn't that hard a trail to follow. Not only was the brush disturbed where they'd both been running, but there were traces of blood on some of the leaves.

Manny's wound appeared to be getting worse.

Grace was about to say something when I held my hand up.

Through the trees, I could see that there was something ahead of us.

It appeared that we'd found them at last.

Chapter 24

As I peered through the brush to get a better look, I saw that Manny was on top of Tyra's back, pinning her to the ground in a small open area among the trees. He was bleeding freely from a scalp wound, and there was a zeal to his expression that gave me cold chills.

I motioned to Grace and whispered, "We have to stop him before he hurts her."

"I'm with you," she said as she picked up a nearby fallen branch. It was a good idea, but I couldn't find one for myself.

I was going to have to go after him the old-fashioned way.

"Let's do this," I said, feeling my blood pumping through me so hard that I thought something in my head was going to explode.

I raced out into the clearing and tackled Manny with everything I had, knocking him off Tyra and ending up rolling on a bit farther myself from the impact.

Tyra was quick. I had to give her credit for that. She was out from under her attacker and on her feet again just as Grace loomed over Manny, a look of triumph on her face as she brandished her branch and threatened to hit him with it.

"You idiots!" Manny yelled at us as he lay there on the ground. "*She's* the one who tried to kill Gabby and set ReNEWed on fire!"

Chapter 25

When I looked over at Tyra, still dazed by Manny's declaration, I saw that there was a revolver in her hands, and it was pointing at the three of us. "Thanks for rescuing me, Suzanne. I wasn't sure how I was going to get out of that one."

"Let them go," Manny said as he struggled to his feet. "Your beef is with me, not them."

It was the most gallant thing he'd probably ever said or done in his life, and I was afraid that there would be no one left alive after this was all over to talk about it.

"They're not going anywhere," she said with a laugh devoid of humanity. "You know, when you think about it, there's not a lot of difference between three bodies and one," she said.

"Why did you do it?" I asked her. "Why did you go after Gabby? Was it because of Manny?"

"That was part of it," she said as she gestured toward Manny. "The truth is that it was mostly about Gabby being so smug about the profit she was making from selling my precious things. When I confronted her about it, she just smiled that sick little grin of hers, like she was so much better than I was. Something in me snapped. I followed her into the back of the store and reached for an iron that was in a box near the door. I couldn't seem to stop myself from hitting her over the head with it. She went down like a sack of grain, and I was certain that I'd killed her. I panicked, found the toaster oven, and then turned it on after putting all kinds of cotton clothing around it. I thought for sure that I'd killed her, and I didn't want anyone to be able to figure out what had happened. I was shocked when I saw that fireman carry her from the building. It was rotten luck for me that she was still alive, and worse yet, now that she's getting her memory back, I have to run, but not before I settle some old scores."

"Manny, you pushed her off the road on *purpose*, didn't you?" Grace asked him.

"She was getting away," he said doggedly. "I couldn't let that happen."

"How did you know that *she* was the one who attacked Gabby and set the fire?" I asked him.

He didn't even get a chance to answer. "I confessed everything to him not fifteen minutes ago, like a fool," Tyra said. "I told him that with Gabby out of the way, we could be together. He rejected me, and called me a sociopath to boot."

Manny shrugged, wincing a little from pain. Evidently the wreck had done more than just cut his forehead. "I told her that I was turning her in, and she said that they'd have to catch her first," Manny interjected.

"So I ran away," Tyra explained. "I would have made it too, but then the idiot hit me with his car and forced me off the road! Can you believe it? And he thinks *I'm* a sociopath!"

Was she honestly trying to justify her behavior to us? The woman was clearly unbalanced. I had to at least agree with Manny about that much.

I heard something in the woods over Tyra's shoulder, but it took everything in my power not to look. Had someone followed us into the woods? If so, I didn't want their lives to be in jeopardy, too. I saw that Grace still had the wooden limb in her hands. I tried to make a suggestion to her with eye movements, but even our close relationship wasn't enough to convey what I was asking her to do.

At least not at first.

Tyra must have seen what I was trying to do, even if Grace hadn't. "Drop that club, Grace," she commanded, pointing her weapon at my friend.

I could see the man moving toward Tyra's back now as he neared her, and it finally became clear who it was.

It was my dear, sweet husband, Jake!

"Look out! She's got a gun!" I shouted out, warning him that Tyra was armed.

"Nice try, Suzanne," Tyra said without looking behind her. "I'm not stupid, you know, and I'm certainly not going to fall for that old trick."

Jake was close enough to strike now.

"I still think it was worth a try," I said, dropping my gaze and trying to act as though I'd been bluffing the entire time.

Tyra let her guard down for just a moment, dropping her aim slightly as she smiled. "Face it. I'm just too smart for you."

"Maybe, maybe not," I said as Jake was finally close enough to make his move.

His reactions were unbelievably quick as he reached out and took the weapon from Tyra's hand before she could stop him. She was clearly shocked as he grabbed her roughly and put a plastic zip-tie around her wrists. "Where did you come from? How could you possibly know we were here?"

"I was driving home, and I saw Suzanne's Jeep parked on the side of the road," he admitted as he kept a hand on her shoulder. "I called Chief Erskine for backup, and then I followed the trail. I heard you all talking, so I circled around so I could get behind you." He then turned to look at me. "Are you okay?"

"Grace and I are fine, but Manny's got a pretty decent cut on his scalp," I said. I looked over at the elder Romeo, who was now pressing a faded green bandana to his forehead. "Thank you, by the way."

"For what?" he asked, looking honestly confused.

"You tried to save us when you thought you were going to die, anyway," I said. "There's still some good in that heart of yours. It's a shame you don't let it show more."

Manny answered with a shrug as we heard sirens coming from the road above us. "That will be Chief Erskine," Jake said.

Tyra tried to get away when she heard that, but Jake wasn't going to let her go anywhere. "Struggle all you want, but I've got you," he told her.

"You should be so lucky," Tyra said in disgust.

I laughed at her response, something that made her even angrier. "You've made yourself a mortal enemy, Suzanne Hart."

"Somehow I'll have to learn to live with the terror of knowing that," I said with a smile.

As Chief Erskine escorted Tyra back up the hill and to his waiting patrol car, she was still staring at me with a glare that would melt ice in winter.

I wasn't worried too much about her, though.

By the time she got out of prison for arson and attempted murder, I had a feeling that I'd be a distant memory for her, and even if it weren't true, I'd take my chances.

After all, I had Jake watching over me, and besides, I was pretty good about looking out for myself, too, when it came right down to it.

If Tyra did decide to come after me, she'd have her hands full.

I would make sure of that.

Chapter 26

G race and I were heading to the Union Square police station to give the chief our statements when I decided to give Gabby a call and catch her up on what had just happened.

"Gabby, we have news," I said as I put my phone on speaker. I was really getting to love that setting. "But first, have you had any luck getting your memory back?"

"No, it's still mostly just one big blank," she said. "I've been getting vague shadows of a few of my memories back since I woke up, but I'm afraid that I'm *never* going to know what really happened in my shop." She sounded so lost that I felt my heart ache for her.

"I can't even imagine how terrible that must be for you, but at least there's something to be happy about. We cracked the case. It was Tyra," I said.

"What? No. Really? *Why?*"

"Apparently she was angry about your profit margins, at least that's what she told us, but I have a feeling that it had more to do with Manny preferring you over her than it was about the money."

"Really? So maybe Manny *wasn't* lying when he said that he loved me after all," Gabby said, the wonder thick in her voice.

"I don't know about that, but Tyra admitted hitting you with an iron from your donation box and then setting ReNEWed on fire to cover up what she'd done. If it matters, she thought that you were already dead when she did it."

"Well, it matters to me," Gabby said, and then she got quiet.

"Gabby, are you okay?" I asked her when there was too much silence for too long on the other end for my taste. "Gabby?"

"It's back!" she said suddenly. "I remember everything now! Suzanne, you did it."

"I didn't do anything," I said, "but even if I did, I didn't do anything by myself. Grace was with me every step of the way."

"Of course I know that. The doctors told me that it could come back in bits and pieces over time, something might trigger my recall unexpectedly, or those particular memories could just be gone forever. I remember Tyra coming back to my shop after our fight. She followed me to the back, and I got tired of her constant whining about how I'd cheated her. I turned my back on her just long enough to pick up the phone to call Chief Grant, and that was the last thing I remember."

"That must have been when she hit you. At least you're safe now."

"What happened to her?" Gabby asked tentatively. "Is she dead?"

"No, she's on her way to the police station even as we speak," I reported. "You don't have to worry about her coming after you anymore. In fact, you can send Bo on home now if you'd like."

"I've got a feeling that I'm stuck with Bo, at least for as long as Penny's still on duty," she said with a hint of laughter in her voice. "He finally got the nerve to ask her out again, and she said yes. His only stipulation was that they couldn't go out until we figured out who tried to kill me."

"And we just did that, didn't we?" I asked her, grinning even though she couldn't see my face.

"You did. You and Grace," Gabby said solemnly. "Thank you. Both of you."

"You're more than welcome," Grace chimed in for the first time.

"You're there, too, Grace? Thanks to you both, then. I don't know how I would have gotten through this without the two of you."

I thought about what had happened over the past few days and how Grace and I had put our lives in jeopardy once again. It was entirely possible that something would have triggered Gabby's memory without any help from us, so it was conceivable that we hadn't needed to do anything.

But would she have recovered those lost moments in time to save her own life?

And then I thought about Manny.

There were a great many things I didn't like about the man, but he'd stepped up when he hadn't had to, and that counted for something, at least in my book. If Grace and I hadn't followed him as he'd chased Tyra down, he would probably be dead now, so our efforts had not been in vain. While it was true that he'd had Tyra pinned to the ground when we'd found them, there was no doubt in my mind that she would have found some way to pull that gun on him and kill him before he could force her out of those woods. Then it would have just been a matter of Tyra waiting patiently and finishing the job she'd started when everyone else let their guards down, and worse yet, she would probably have gotten away with two murders in the process, and none of us would have been the wiser. If we hadn't kept pressuring her in the first place, Tyra probably wouldn't have acted so rashly with Manny, so it was entirely possible that the attempted murder and arson would have gone unpunished, with Gabby's murder following soon after to make sure that one last loose thread was severed forever.

"You're most welcome," Grace said. "When are they going to let you out of there?"

"They want to keep me one more night for observation, but we'll have to see about that," Gabby said with great confidence. I didn't doubt her ability to talk herself into an early discharge, and clearly she didn't question it herself.

"Have you had any more time to think about what comes next, Gabby?" I asked her.

She paused for a few moments, and then she said, "Like I said before, I'm going to step back and take a little time to figure things out. My insurance will cover the shop and everything in it. I was always careful about being fully covered, so I don't have to worry about money for the rest of my life, as long as I'm careful with it. Honestly, I'm not really sure what I'm going to do, but that's the beauty of it, Suzanne. I don't *have* to know this very second."

After we got back into town, Grace asked me to drop her off at the police station. She wanted to check in with Stephen, and I couldn't blame her. I'd spoken briefly with Jake at the Union Square police station, and we'd agreed to catch up at home again.

As I waited there for him, I tried to decide how I was going to approach what I had to say to him. I didn't want him to think that I was pushing him away, but I had to tell him that he belonged in law enforcement and that he couldn't turn his back on it a minute more.

If that meant that we'd have to make sacrifices, then so be it.

I knew that I was lucky to have him in my life, luckier than even I realized at times, but I couldn't keep him at home anymore.

He had to find his purpose in life again, and I was determined to do whatever I could to make sure that he found it.

Chapter 27

"Suzanne, I've decided what I want to do with the rest of my life," Jake said as he burst into the cottage. "Hear me out, okay?"

"Sure," I said, realizing that this was getting to be a habit for him, insisting that I not comment until he was finished with what he had to say. What was that about? Was I getting to be a little too chatty for him?

"This case told me that my particular set of skills is needed out there, so I'm going to keep consulting, but I'm not going back to work full time," he said. "I've done that before, and I can't stand the grind. I was just getting the toughest cases when I was an inspector, and it was getting harder and harder on me. Frankly, I don't need the pressure, but if I consult, taking cases every now and then only when something intrigues me, then the way I see it, it's the best of both worlds. Sure, I'll have to be away every now and then, but never for long periods of time, and I can turn down any job I don't want to take. Besides, we could use the extra money, but that's not really why I want to do it. I felt alive solving those robberies, but part of it was because it was *my* choice to do it, and not because I was taking orders from a boss. I've seen enough of how you live your life at the donut shop to realize that I want to be the one in control of my own destiny. It's worth more to me than any paycheck or insurance plan could ever be." He stared at me a moment and then asked, "What do you think?"

"First of all, I don't think I *ever* want to hear you tell me that I have to hear you out without interrupting," I said, scolding him a bit. "We're a team, remember?"

"You're right. I'm sorry," he said, clearly regretting his earlier behavior. "I just really want this, and I wanted you to hear everything before you weighed in. I agree though, it's a bad habit, and I give you my word that it's the last time I'll ever do it. From here on out, feel free to say whatever you'd like to me, any time you want."

"How gracious of you," I said, adding a quick smile to show him that I was just teasing. "As to your statement, I am in full agreement with everything you just said. In fact, I was trying to figure out a way to convince you that this would be perfect for you and that you *had* to keep consulting. I don't want you to be a state police inspector ever again, but you need *something* in your life, and I think consulting is perfect. It's especially true since you've had time to step away from your old job and be able to remember what you loved about the work in the first place. I'm very excited for you."

"I'm excited for me, too," he said as he wrapped me up in his arms and hugged me fiercely.

I felt bad for the women Manny Wright had led astray with promises of love and the empty spaces they must have felt in their hearts to need to hear them so much. I completely understood the desire to be loved after what I'd gone through with Max, and even though I knew that I didn't have to have a man in my life to make me happy, I also realized that when it was right, it made everything better.

Then again, if I'd had to deal with any more Maxes, I probably would *still* be single, but I'd found the perfect man, not necessarily for every woman out there, but for me, and I was never going to take that for granted.

Life was just too short to treat something so special any other way.

RECIPES

Lemon Candy Drop Donuts

O ne day I was looking around for something to use to add some zip to my normal lemon-flavored donuts, and I happened upon a bag of hard lemon candy drops. After all, they are tart and sweet, and they offer the unmistakable taste of lemon, so I thought, why not?

The first batch I made, I didn't crush the candies fine enough. With the second batch, they were closer to powder, which worked but lacked a bit of crackle when they were bitten into. The third batch, like Goldilocks and the Three Bears, turned out to be just right. Even if you're not fond of hard candies, don't be afraid to smash them up thoroughly and use them in your batter. You can also reserve a little and sprinkle this tart, sugary powder on top of your donuts, whether you ice them first or not. I double-baggie three or four lemon candy drops and smash them with a rolling pin to crush them to the size I like. By the way, this step is *very* therapeutic!

Ingredients

1 cup flour, unbleached all-purpose

2 tablespoons crushed lemon hard candies

1 teaspoon baking powder

1/4 teaspoon lemon peel, grated

1 dash salt

1/2 cup whole milk

1/3 cup granulated sugar

4 tablespoons butter, melted

1 egg, beaten

2 teaspoons lemon juice, freshly squeezed

1/2 vanilla bean, scraped

Directions

In a bowl, mix the flour, crushed lemon candy, baking powder, lemon peel, and salt until everything is thoroughly incorporated. In another bowl, combine the whole milk, sugar, butter, egg, lemon juice, and the vanilla bean seeds.

Mix this well, and then slowly add the dry ingredients into the wet until they are combined, being careful not to overmix, as this could cause denser donuts.

Bake these donuts in a 375°F oven or in your donut maker for 6 to 8 minutes, then remove them to a cooling rack. You can make a simple lemon glaze using melted sugar, lemon juice, and a little grated lemon peel, or dust them immediately with powdered confectioners' sugar and then sprinkle on a little of the leftover crushed hard lemon candy.

Yields 8 to 10 donuts.

Peanut Brittle

Okay, I know it's not a donut, but I've been known to branch out to other treats as well, and this certainly qualifies. In the future, I'm thinking about incorporating some finely broken-up brittle into my next peanut donuts, so if it works out, I'll keep you posted.

A word of warning about this recipe. Peanut brittle is best made by adults, and adults only. I've *never* made it with children nearby, and I wouldn't recommend it. We are dealing with some very hot temperatures here, and melted sugar can burn, and burn fiercely, so be extremely careful, especially when moving it from the pot onto the cookie sheet. I'm not trying to scare you off from making this delightful treat, but you should be aware that it isn't without an element of risk, so consider yourself warned.

Ingredients

1 cup whole granulated sugar

1/2 cup light corn syrup

1/8 teaspoon common table salt

1 cup dry roasted lightly salted peanuts, shelled

2 tablespoons butter, salted or unsalted both work here

1 1/2 teaspoons vanilla extract

1 teaspoon baking soda

Directions

Combine sugar, corn syrup, and table salt in a medium-sized heavy saucepan. Heat over medium heat, stirring constantly, until the mixture starts to boil. Let it boil without stirring approximately 5 minutes, or until a candy thermometer reads 300 to 304 degrees, depending on the doneness preferred.

Add the peanuts, and then continue to cook for 2 to 3 minutes until it reaches 280 degrees (the peanuts will cool the mixture down when they are added). Remove the pan from the heat and stir in the butter, vanilla extract, and baking soda. Be careful here. The baking soda reacts with the mixture, causing it to bubble up. This is what lightens the brittle enough to allow you to eat it without breaking your teeth, so don't skip this step!

Carefully pour this mixture out onto a buttered baking sheet and spread it out with a spatula that's been coated with cooking spray.

Allow it to cool for an hour, and then break it apart and enjoy.

Brittle can be stored in an airtight container to make it last, but I've never personally tried it myself, since it never lasts that long around my house!

Spicy Lemon-Orange Donuts

One of the many reasons I love the holiday season is the opportunity to pull out all of the stops and make delightful treats without guilt. Okay, without too much, anyway! This is an exquisite donut recipe that can easily be converted to muffins. Give it a try. It's a real winner, at least in my house, and as an added bonus, it makes my house smell like Christmas any time of year!

Ingredients

1 cup granulated sugar

1 cup milk (2% or whole will do nicely)

2 egg yolks only, beaten

1/2 stick butter (1/4 cup) melted

2 tablespoons orange extract

2 tablespoons lemon juice, freshly squeezed

1 1/2 tablespoons canola oil

1 1/2 teaspoons cinnamon

The zest of one orange, finely grated

The zest of one lemon, finely grated

Candy orange slice wedges, cut into small pieces

3–4 cups flour

1 tablespoon baking powder

Directions

Mix the sugar, milk, egg yolks, melted butter, orange extract, lemon juice, canola oil, cinnamon, orange zest, and lemon zest. Sift the flour and baking powder together in a different bowl. If preferred (and I heartily recommend it), cut and add candy orange slice wedges and mix into the dry ingredients until combined well. Then add the dry ingredients to the wet, stirring well as you go. This will make a very stiff dough.

Chill the dough for at least 1 hour, then turn it onto a floured surface. Knead it into a ball, and then roll the ball out to 1/2 to 1/4 inches thick. This may look a little lumpy, depending on if you used the candy wedges. Cut out the rounds.

Heat enough canola oil to fry the donuts at 375°F, and then add the donut rounds and cook for 2 minutes on each side, being sure not to crowd the donuts in the pot as they cook. Drain them on a cooling rack, and then dust them with powdered sugar or eat them plain.

Makes approximately 1 dozen donuts.

If you enjoy Jessica Beck Mysteries and you would like to be notified when the next book is being released, please visit our website at jessicabeckmysteries.net for valuable information about Jessica's books, and sign up for her new-releases-only mail blast.

Your email address will not be shared, sold, bartered, traded, broadcast, or disclosed in any way. There will be no spam from us, just a friendly reminder when the latest book is being released, and of course, you can drop out at any time.

Other Books by Jessica Beck

The Donut Mysteries
Glazed Murder
Fatally Frosted
Sinister Sprinkles
Evil Éclairs
Tragic Toppings
Killer Crullers
Drop Dead Chocolate
Powdered Peril
Illegally Iced
Deadly Donuts
Assault and Batter
Sweet Suspects
Deep Fried Homicide
Custard Crime
Lemon Larceny
Bad Bites
Old Fashioned Crooks
Dangerous Dough
Troubled Treats
Sugar Coated Sins
Criminal Crumbs
Vanilla Vices

Raspberry Revenge
Fugitive Filling
Devil's Food Defense
Pumpkin Pleas
Floured Felonies
Mixed Malice
Tasty Trials
Baked Books
Cranberry Crimes
Boston Cream Bribes
Cherry Filled Charges
Scary Sweets
Cocoa Crush
Pastry Penalties
Apple Stuffed Alibies
Perjury Proof
Caramel Canvas
Dark Drizzles
Counterfeit Confections
Measured Mayhem
Blended Bribes
The Classic Diner Mysteries
A Chili Death
A Deadly Beef
A Killer Cake
A Baked Ham
A Bad Egg
A Real Pickle
A Burned Biscuit
The Ghost Cat Cozy Mysteries
Ghost Cat: Midnight Paws
Ghost Cat 2: Bid for Midnight

The Cast Iron Cooking Mysteries
Cast Iron Will
Cast Iron Conviction
Cast Iron Alibi
Cast Iron Motive
Cast Iron Suspicion
Nonfiction
The Donut Mysteries Cookbook

Made in the
USA
Monee, IL